Peppermint Proposal

A River's End Ranch Story

Kirsten Osbourne

Sign up for instant notification of all of Kirsten's New Releases Text 'BOB' to 42828

And

For a complete list of Kirsten's works head to her website wwww.kirstenandmorganna.com

This book is dedicated to Joannie Kley. I hope you never stop reading!

Chapter One

Max Logan concentrated on the road as he navigated the narrow mountain roads leading to River's End Ranch. His boss, Adam McClain, had sent him off on a month of paid time off, so he was going to visit his foster brother, Kevin, in the frozen northland of Idaho. It was a far cry from Texas, for certain.

As he drove the narrow roads, snow began again. He'd spent several hours in a blizzard in Colorado, so it was only logical he'd hit another snowstorm in Idaho. He'd planned to take two days for the drive up, but the two had turned into four because he had to keep pulling over. Texas boys were not taught how to drive in the snow as a matter of course, unlike most of the rest of the country. And they certainly weren't taught to drive in the mountains during snowstorms. Mountains were hard enough without snow!

As he drove, he let his mind wander. He'd lived on the McClain Boys' Ranch since he was fourteen years old, and his mother had decided he was too unmanageable to keep around. At first, he'd hated the ranch and everything about it, including the sons of the family who ran the ranch. They'd had stupid names after some boys in a movie, which made them all stupid to his way of thinking.

And then something had happened after he'd been there for about two months. He realized he was no longer living to get in trouble. Instead, he was looking forward to the hard work they did at the ranch. He went to school all day, and studied and did chores all night. But the people at the ranch genuinely cared about him. It had been strange, but he'd gradually started to think of the place as home. When it had come time to get a job and move on, he'd gotten a job and moved—but he'd moved into the bunkhouse on the ranch property, and his job had been as a cowboy there at the ranch.

For the past five years, he'd lived in a small cabin on the property that had been built by the original orphan boys who'd made their homes at the ranch. It wasn't big and spacious, but it was perfect for a single cowboy like him.

He felt like he owed the McClains so much after the way they'd treated him that he had never thought to use his vacation days. He'd sign up for them, but he'd work somewhere around the ranch anyway. That was why Adam, the oldest brother who now ran the ranch, had told him he was leaving the ranch for a full month. He had the vacation days saved up, and he was going to take them if it killed him.

Thinking long and hard about where he wanted to go, he'd settled on a trip to Idaho to see Kevin, who had become a pastor. He'd written awesome things about the destination ranch he now worked for—doing weddings and holding Sunday services—and Max had found himself intrigued.

He passed a sign that said Riston was only twenty miles away. With as hard as it was snowing, that would be a blessing. Kevin had arranged for him to have one of the cabins at the ranch, and he found himself getting more and more excited as he drove. He hadn't seen Kevin since his last trip home, which had been what? Five years before? It would be good to see his favorite brother.

He followed the GPS until he reached a sign that said, "River's End Ranch," and he turned in the drive. The first building he saw was Kelsey's Kafé, and he stopped in their parking lot. He needed a cup of hot coffee and some lunch. He'd call Kevin as soon as he ordered—because food was more imperative than seeing his brother—and then he'd figure out where to go next.

Leaving his pick-up truck in the small parking lot in front of the café, he hurried inside, hoping Kevin would have some warm clothes he could borrow. The men had always been close to the same size, so he was sure he could wear whatever Kevin had. He hadn't really thought things out well when he'd left Texas. Seventy degrees in Texas had quickly turned into twenty degrees in Idaho. He would have to take some time to get used to the cold.

Rubbing his arms briskly—he hadn't even thought to buy a coat—he looked around the café and spotted a booth in one corner, sliding into it. He grabbed a menu and glanced at it, hoping someone would come see him soon. That coffee was a necessity with as cold as he was.

A leggy blond in a pink uniform approached him. "Hi, I'm Joni. You new here?"

Max nodded. "I'm here to visit my brother."

She tilted her head to one side and pursed her lips. "Who would that brother be?"

"Kevin Roberts."

Her face lit up. "Oh, Pastor Kevin! We're happy to have you here. Do you want to hear the specials?"

"I just drove here from Texas with no winter coat. I think more than anything, I need a cup of coffee."

She nodded. "I'll get the coffee and then come back and tell you the specials. Bob made gumbo today, and that will warm you through and through."

"Get me some gumbo with that coffee, would you?" Max was certain no one could make gumbo as well as his foster mother, Lillian, but even bad gumbo would warm him up a bit.

She grinned. "I'll be right back!"

Max watched her go, admiring the way her backside moved in her awful uniform. If she was an example of what they had here at the ranch, he'd be happy to stay for a bit. He pulled his phone from his pocket and tapped Kevin's number. "Hey, it's Max."

"Max! Did you make it in? When I saw it start snowing this morning, I got a little worried you wouldn't make it today either."

"I'm sitting in Kelsey's Kafé. A very pretty blonde is walking toward me with a cup of coffee and a bowl of gumbo." He winked at the blonde, who blushed just a bit.

"I can't get away until this evening. Have lunch, then go to the main house. They'll tell you where your cabin is," Kevin told him. "I'll come see you as soon as I can get away."

"What are you busy doing? It's not Sunday!" Max was well aware that pastors didn't only work on Sundays, but he had to rib his long-time friend.

Kevin laughed softly. "I have a wedding tomorrow, and we're going over vows and doing a quick rehearsal."

Max frowned. Kevin wouldn't have time for him the next day either! "All right. Well, come see me when you find a minute."

"Explore the ranch. It's an amazing place."

"I might do that." Max pressed the end button on his phone, not wanting to disturb Kevin any longer. He wasn't sure why he had in his head that his brother would only work a few hours a week, but he was obviously wrong.

He smiled at the waitress who was waiting for him to finish his call. "What did you say your name was?"

"Joni Kley."

"Okay, Joni, tell me the specials. Looks like I've got some time to kill. Kevin is doing a wedding tomorrow, and they're going over vows and stuff today."

Joni slid into the booth across from him. "I hope you don't mind. I've been pulling double duty this week. I'm assistant manager, and the manager's twins have been sick."

"How old are the twins?"

"Nine months. They're girls and as adorable as can be." Joni grinned. "If you're here for a little while, I'm sure you'll meet them. They're the grandbabies of the people who owned the ranch until just recently, when they deeded it to their six kids."

Max smiled. "Sounds like I need to meet them."

"Okay, sorry to ramble. Specials today are Jambalaya and Bob's ribeye. Both are fabulous. Ribeye comes with baked potato and salad. Jambalaya comes with just salad. Can't go wrong whatever you choose. Bob is an amazing chef, but don't ever let him know I said that!"

A man with a chef's hat and an ornery look on his face stuck his head out of the kitchen. "I heard that, and I'll *never* let you forget it!"

Joni made a face. "He won't either. He's a pain in my behind, and if he wasn't such a great cook, I don't know how any of us would put up with him."

Max laughed. "That's Bob, I take it?"

"Yeah. His wife runs the bakery in the Old West town. Have you been there yet?" Joni loved the historical section of the ranch.

"No, I got to the ranch and saw the café. The café meant the siren song of coffee was calling my name, so I came on in."

Joni grinned. "Do you want a few minutes to look over the menu? Or do you want one of the specials?"

"I'll take the jambalaya and another bowl of gumbo." He pushed his coffee cup toward her. "And more coffee."

She slid out of the booth. "Give me a minute, and I'll have it for you."

"How late is this place open?" he asked.

Joni glanced at her watch. "Another thirty minutes. We close at two."

"I better hurry then!"

She shook her head. "Nah. I'm closing up today, so you just take your time. I'm out of school now, so there's nothing to rush home to." She had to figure out what she was going to do with her life, but for now, she was content to help Kelsi out. Soon.

"All right." He took out his phone and checked messages as she rushed away. He was the last customer in the place, and he felt guilty making her stay, but it would take him too long to check in and find where he was staying. His food would get cold if he got it to go.

Five minutes later, he had the jambalaya in front of him, along with gumbo and another cup of coffee. He was thrilled, because he was hungry, and it was doing a lot to warm him up. He watched as Bob left the café, and then Joni came over and sat down in his booth again. She had a box with little packets of sugar, and she had all the little sugar containers from the tables. "You mind a little company?"

He shook his head. "A man would have to be stupid to turn you down. You mentioned school. What did you go to school for?" He hadn't gone to college himself, because he went to work for the McClains right after school. He was happy, but he wondered how his life would be different.

"Social work. I graduated in May, but I'm still working here. I thought I'd give Kelsi time to get her feet under her with the new babies before I left, but she's pretty much done that. It's time for me to start job hunting."

"Social work? Are you tied to the area, or are you willing to move? Kevin and I were raised on a boys' ranch. Adam's always looking for good social workers."

"Adam?"

"He's the oldest biological son of the couple who has run the ranch for years." Max sat back, running his fingers through his hair that had been mussed by his cowboy hat. He wasn't sure why he wore one away from the ranch, except that he felt naked without it. "Well, kind of. The boys' ranch was run by the McClain family, and Adam is the oldest of the McClain boys. I was sent there because I was a bit more incorrigible than your average teenage felon."

She laughed. "Did you like it there?"

He nodded. "It's an amazing place. I still live and work there sixteen years later. I have a little house on the ranch now, and I can't imagine living anywhere else."

"And this ranch is where?" Joni had only ever lived in Idaho, but she was open to living elsewhere. Especially if they grew men like the one across from her.

"Texas hill country. Most beautiful stretch of land on God's green earth."

"More beautiful than River's End? I don't think that's possible!" Joni would have to take him out on the ranch so he could see what a truly beautiful place he was visiting. The view from up in the mountains was absolutely breathtaking.

He shrugged. "Beautiful in a different way. I don't know if I could leave it now. The ranch is run by the seven sons of the family. There always seem to be seven sons who run it, and they're the sons of the youngest brother of the previous generation. It's a bit spooky, if you ask me." Max had never delved too deeply into the oddity of the family he worked for, because he was afraid he might really be creeped out by what he'd find.

"Do you ever see your parents?" she asked.

He shook his head. "No, my mother didn't want to see me. I caused too many problems for her." He shrugged. "Sometimes I wonder what it would be like to see her again, but then I remember that she washed her hands of me." He was glad he'd found a family who loved him so quickly after leaving home, but it still stung that his birth parents hadn't wanted him. Of course, he hadn't exactly been a model child.

Joni wanted to ask what he did that was so terrible, but she didn't think it would be a good idea. "That's sad. I can't imagine doing that to a child of mine."

He shrugged. "I messed up. That was the end of it for her."

"But you were happy where you ended up?"

He nodded. "I really ended up exactly where I needed to be, which was hard to believe when I got there. I really felt like I was surrounded by love for the first time in my life." He remembered grandparents who had seemed to loved him, but he hadn't seen them since he was five. If they'd really loved him, wouldn't they have made an effort?

"That's really cool." She smiled. "That's the kind of work I want to do, and it's why I got my degree in social work."

"Well, if you're willing to move to Texas, I'm sure I could arrange an interview with Adam." He found himself wishing she'd agree. There was something about her. He definitely wanted to get to know her better.

She bit her lip, thinking about it. "I might be willing to interview, but it's so far away." She wasn't sure she could live outside of the mountains of Idaho, though. They were in her blood. Her family had lived in Idaho for three generations.

"Adam only interviews in person, so you can't just do it over Skype. He says he can't get a read on people the same way if they're not in the same room with him, whatever that means." Again, he was afraid to ask. The McClains were just odd.

"I totally understand that. I get a better feel for people in person as well. I think that's pretty normal."

"I guess." He finished his jambalaya and pushed his plate away. "Now I need to figure out where the main house is, whatever that means." He hoped she could at least draw him a map. Finding his way around the huge ranch might be confusing.

"Give me a minute to shove your dishes in the dishwasher and start it, and I'll ring you up and walk over to the main house with you." She jumped to her feet and grabbed his dishes, hurrying into the kitchen with them. When she came back, she rang him up, accepting his card. "All right, let's walk over."

"You don't have to do that. I'm sure you've got lots of other things you'd rather be doing." He'd heard the service on the ranch was exceptional, but she was taking it a step further than he'd expected.

She shrugged. "I love showing people the ranch. Besides, I'm pretty much alone right now. I'll probably do karaoke at the restaurant tonight, but those are my only plans for the day. Kevin and Bridget usually go too."

"Do I have to sing if I go to karaoke night?"

She shook her head. "Not if you don't want to."

"Do you sing?"

"Sometimes. I enjoy singing, but it depends on my mood."

"Well, I probably won't sing, but I sure will enjoy my time listening to others. Maybe we can get Kevin up there!"

"Pastor Kevin sings? Really?"

"Oh, there's a lot you don't know about him. We had barbecues every Friday night, and he would always sing. I don't know how they talked him into it, but he was *really* good. Sang all the old Garth Brooks songs. I've never heard anyone with as much natural talent as he had, and he wanted to be a pastor. I'll never get it!"

"I guess there's no way to understand what's in other people's minds. If he loves what he does, then we should all be happy. I can't believe he never sings for karaoke night. They always go, and they sit and talk and hold hands. They usually go with Bridget's twin, Kaya, and her husband, Glen."

"I haven't had the pleasure of meeting Bridget yet. Is she nice?" Max found he was very curious about Kevin's wife.

"Nice?" Joni thought about it for a moment. How could she describe Bridget accurately? "Bridget is very nice, but she's...different than anyone you've ever met. I think you'll like her."

"I'm sure if she loves Kevin and treats him right, I'll like her just fine. Does she work here at the ranch?" He was surprised how little he knew about Kevin's wife.

"She runs the first-aid station. She's a nurse." Joni had always liked Bridget, but she was very odd. No one loved arguing about Disney princesses half as much as Bridget did.

Max visibly shivered, rubbing his arms. "How far to the main house?"

"We're almost there. Where's your coat?"

He shrugged. "I don't even *have* a winter coat. I have a jacket I use in the winter, but it's soaked through. It was warmer without it. We don't really wear winter coats in Texas. If I need something heavier than a light jacket, I just wear a sweatshirt underneath and keep on going."

"Really? I can't imagine." Joni shook her head. "I've always lived in Idaho, and it gets cold here in the winter. We'll have to take you to the general store later so you can get yourself a coat."

"General store?"

She nodded. "We have an Old West town here, and there's a general store. It's laid out like an old-fashioned general store, but you can get just about everything you need there."

"Oh, good. I thought I was going to have to steal some of Kevin's clothes."

Joni grinned. "He probably wouldn't mind. There are other options, though. Do you know where you're staying?"

"One of the cabins, he said. I let Kevin choose the place for me. I trust him."

"He's a good man to trust." She put her hand on the door to go into the main house, but he opened it for her. She walked to the front desk and smiled. "Hi, Natasha. This is Max. He's Pastor Kevin's brother, and he's going to stay in one of the cabins for a bit." She looked at Max. "How long are you here for anyway?"

"About a month."

Natasha grabbed a key. "This will open your front and back doors." She pulled out a map and circled a square on it. "You're here, but you want to go to your cabin, which is here. Follow the road around."

Max nodded, taking the key and the map. "Thank you."

"Do you want to put a credit card on file for incidentals?"

He pulled a card from his wallet and handed it to her. "Can I charge meals to my room?"

"In the restaurant you can, but not in the café. We have too many locals eating there for it to be practical." Natasha handed him a few brochures. "This will explain everything we do here at the ranch. I hope you'll enjoy your stay."

Max eyed Joni. "I have a feeling I'm going to love it here."

Chapter Two

Joni rode with Max, directing him to the cabin. "I really think you should stop off at the general store first. You're going to freeze to death otherwise. You need gloves, a coat, and a hat, minimum."

He frowned at her. "I have a hat."

"I mean a winter hat, not a cowboy hat. You look—" She stopped there, realizing she'd been just about to tell him that he looked great in his cowboy hat. What was wrong with her? "I think it would be prudent to get yourself something to keep you warm, not just to look good."

"You do know that cowboys wear their hats for a real purpose, right? It's not *just* to look good. Without my hat, my face and neck would burn from the hot Texas sun. I *need* this hat."

"Not in Idaho, you don't. I'm not sure if you realize that you left Texas days ago. It's time for you to try to acclimate and dress like the natives dress. Or you can freeze to death."

He frowned at her. "I'm sure my cabin will be warm."

"Yes, it will. You're planning on staying inside for an entire month? You won't go outside to go to the diner? You won't go to karaoke tonight to urge Pastor Kevin to sing? You won't go snowmobiling or go on a sleigh ride?"

He sighed. "I guess I need warm winter gear to do all that. Though, I think I could wait until tomorrow."

"If you don't go straight to the general store you'll have to. They close at four, and it's getting close to that now." She'd been with him for a couple of hours, which was surprising. Usually if she was around a man for more than twenty minutes, she was bored out of her mind.

"Fine. How do I get to this general store?"

She directed him to the store, where Heidi would sell him everything he needed for the winter. His cowboy boots wouldn't be a lot of protection against the cold. She made a note to start harassing him about those as soon as he'd picked out a coat. She had no idea if he had the money to buy the things he needed, but she was sure Heidi would let him use her employee discount if it came to that.

Once they were inside, she helped him pick out a thick, heavy coat that would actually keep him warm. Then she found a pair of gloves. "Now for the boots."

"Boots! I *have* boots."

"You have boots that are perfect for chasing down calves and riding horses. I'm talking about boots that are good for snowmobiling and hiking in the snow." Joni crossed her arms over her chest, glaring at him. "If you don't keep your feet warm, you'll catch your death of cold. And then Bridget will have to take care of you and nurse you back to health, and Kevin will be mad at you because you kept his wife away from him."

"Are you sure you studied to be a social worker and not a writer? Cuz those tales you're telling me sure do sound like you're practicing making up stories."

"Boots."

Heidi walked over then, looking back and forth between the two of them, a huge grin on her face. "Introduce me, Joni. I didn't know you were seeing anyone!"

Joni made a face. "I'm not! He came into the diner a couple of hours ago. He's Pastor Kevin's brother."

Heidi looked at him for a moment. "I don't see a resemblance."

Max had to laugh. "I'm half-Mexican, and he's as white as white can be. We're foster brothers."

"I see." Heidi turned to the display of boots. "Joni's right. You need something that will keep your feet warm or you'll get sick. It's too cold to run around without proper protection on your feet."

"It's only November!" Max protested.

Heidi and Joni exchanged a look. "We had our first snowfall in mid-September," Joni told him. "You're not in Texas anymore, Toto."

"Apparently not." He sighed, giving in and looking at the boot display. He saw a pair of fur-lined hiking boots. "Will these work?"

Heidi nodded. "What size?" Once she had her answer, she hurried off to the back room to find the right boots for him.

Max looked at Joni standing beside him. "She assumed we were a couple."

Joni shrugged. "This ranch is known for matching people up. We even have a semi-crazy old lady who feeds people snickerdoodles, talks to fairies, and pushes people together every chance she gets."

"Why does she do that?" he asked, frowning.

"Which thing?"

"Any of it! Doesn't she think that if people want to get together, they can figure it out on their own?"

"I'm sure she doesn't think so. I've not been part of her matchmaking before, but I've seen enough of it to know she feels like she's extremely vital to every one of the matches." Joni picked up a hat and handed it to him. "You can wear your cowboy hat over it, but make sure you have that on to keep your head warm."

"Why do you want me to wear my cowboy hat over it? You like how I look in my hat, don't you?" Max's eyes danced with amusement. She was sweet, and he'd already figured out that she blushed when she was teased too much. He would enjoy exploiting that fact.

Joni blushed, turning from him. "You're being a pain, Tex."

He grinned, hurrying in front of her and tapping his index finger against her nose. "I am just calling things as I see them. That's how we do things in Texas, you know."

Heidi came back with the boots in his size, insisting he try them on. "I want to make sure they fit you right before you walk out of here with them." She looked over at Joni. "Are you going to karaoke tonight?"

Joni nodded. "I plan on it. I'm enjoying having a little more free-time."

"I'm sure you are! As long as I've known you, you've had your face buried in a schoolbook. Now you're working like a crazy woman for Kelsi. How are the twins? Have you heard?" Everyone on the ranch felt they had a vested interest in the first grandbabies of the next Weston generation.

"The sheriff came in at lunch. He said they were mostly better, but Kelsi felt like she wanted them home from daycare for one more day. So I'll run the diner tomorrow, and she'll be back Monday." Kelsi was the youngest of the Weston siblings, and she'd married the sheriff, Shane Clapper.

"Oh, good. I hate that they got so sick. When are Wilber and Bobbi due back? Have you heard?"

"They'll be here the Wednesday before for Thanksgiving. Bobbi said she was going to be here from Thanksgiving through New Year's. I think that's a little over a month, but she wants to be with her grandbabies for their first holiday season. You can't blame her for that."

Heidi shook her head. "Sure can't. She's so in love with her grandbabies, it's almost comical."

"It would be impossible to not love those two sweethearts!" Joni looked at Max, who was standing wearing the snow boots. "How do they fit?"

"They feel tight, but I think they're supposed to. They're warm." He took a few steps in them. "I think they'll work for outdoor activities." Looking at Joni, he frowned. "I think since you forced me to come in here and get all suited up for winter, you owe me a tour of the ranch. Tomorrow?"

Joni shook her head. "I have to work tomorrow. I can do it after church on Sunday."

He grinned. "Sounds good to me."

"Have you ever ridden a snowmobile?"

Max shook his head. "Anything like a four-wheeler?" When he'd been a teenager, they'd done some four-wheeling on the ranch, all of them ending up covered in mud and laughing. Peter, Adam's father, had always laughed, but Lillian would get annoyed with the extra work it caused her.

"I guess a little." Joni hadn't really had the opportunity to ride either very much. She'd always studied harder than anyone else she knew, and that kept her from having a lot of fun outdoors. Her schooling mattered to her, though.

"I'm in. Do you go to church here on the ranch? I can take you to lunch after, and then we can explore."

"Sounds good to me." She felt her heart racing a little. Was he asking her out? Or were they just going as friends? Either way, she was determined to have fun.

"What time is karaoke tonight?" he asked, gathering all of his purchases and carrying them to the counter where Heidi rang them up. He winced when Heidi gave him his total, but he paid with cash.

"Seven. If we go to the restaurant at six, we'll have good seats."

"I'll text Kevin and see if he and Bridget will join us."

Joni realized they were talking as if it was a given that they'd go together, but she wanted to go with him, so she said nothing. It would have been nice if he'd asked, but men rarely did what she wanted them to do.

"Sounds good." She still wasn't sure what to make of Bridget, but she could spend the evening with her. With a wave to Heidi, she headed for his truck. "Do you want me to meet you at the restaurant?"

He frowned. "Why don't you come to my cabin, and we'll go over together." He wanted others to know she was with him. He wasn't sure why, because he'd never felt possessive of anyone before, but there was something special about her.

"Sounds good. I can be there about quarter 'til six? Then we can walk over—or drive, if you can't handle the cold." Joni hid her grin. She didn't know why she was challenging him, but she sure did enjoy it.

"If you can handle it, I can handle it." He wanted to tell her that he'd love to see her in the heat of Texas and see how quickly she melted, but he was trying to be a gentleman. Lillian, his foster mother, had drilled it into him from an early age that you acted like a gentleman in the presence of a lady. Period. There were no exceptions to the rule.

"You're on." She climbed into the passenger seat of his truck and gave him directions to his cabin. "There's a hot tub out back if you feel like soaking for a bit."

"Do people really get into hot tubs in the winter?"

She laughed. "There's no other time to do it!"

He shook his head. "You're going to make sure I experience Idaho, aren't you?" He wasn't sure he was ready to pretend to be a polar bear. Did they have polar bears in Idaho?

"You're only here for a month. I think a crash course is going to be necessary."

He sighed. "I'm going to be the best displaced Texan in Idaho you've ever seen! I promise you that!"

AFTER UNPACKING, MAX called Kevin again, thankful to find him alone this time. "Can we do karaoke at the restaurant tonight?"

"Sure. Bridget and I love karaoke."

"So why is it no one around here talks about the fabulous crooning of Pastor Kevin?" Max couldn't wait to hear Kevin's answer to that. Driving Kevin crazy had been one of his favorite pastimes for over a decade.

Kevin sighed. "Who have you been talking to?"

"Joni. The girl who works at the café."

"What did you tell her?"

"Just that you sound like Garth Brooks when you sing, and I was never sure why you'd chosen to be a pastor when you could be a singer." Max grinned, knowing he'd gotten Kevin's goat. It wasn't easy to do either.

"Fine. Don't tell anyone else, okay?"

"Why not? You're hiding your light under a bushel. Aren't you supposed to use your talents for God?"

"I'll see you there. What time?" Kevin sounded exasperated, and Max pumped his fist in the air.

"Six. Does that work?"

"Sure. Six is good."

"If you get there before us, get a table for four, would you?"

"Yeah. Who's the fourth?"

Max pretended not to hear and ended the call. He'd almost forgotten just how much he enjoyed bothering the unflappable Kevin. He'd missed his friend.

JONI WENT THROUGH HER closet four times before she found just the right outfit to wear that night. Karaoke was always casual, but she couldn't be casual the first time she went out with Max. Whether he thought it was a date or not, she was going to look at it that way!

She found just the right pair of jeans, and a silk blouse. Spending more time than usual in front of a mirror, she actually put make-up on and styled her hair. She couldn't remember the last time she'd done that.

When she felt like she was ready, she took one last look in the mirror before hurrying out to her car, not bothering to lock the door. The town was small enough that she knew everyone. She wasn't even a little bit worried about anyone breaking in.

She drove the short distance to the ranch and straight to Max's rental cabin. When she got to the door, she knocked quickly, hoping he was ready. She wasn't sure if she would be too nervous to talk to him if she had to wait. Why he made her nervous, she didn't know. Oh, wait. Yes, she did. It was because he was unbelievably sexy.

He opened the door, dressed for the night. He was wearing his cowboy hat instead of the knit cap she'd talked him into buying, but they wouldn't be outside for too long. Besides, she really did like how he looked in his cowboy hat. He was wearing jeans, his winter boots, and the heavy winter coat she'd helped him choose.

"You ready?"

He nodded, stepping outside. "Yup. I'm ready. I've been singing all evening, getting my voice warmed up."

She grinned. "So you're going to sing, are you?"

He shrugged. "I might be talked into it." He glanced down at her, smiling at the way she looked with her hands tucked deep into her pockets and her shoulders hunched against the cold. "What about you? Are you singing?"

"Maybe." She wouldn't though. She never had and she never would. She knew she sounded like a wounded bear when she sang, and no one would get her to sing in public. "Are Pastor Kevin and Bridget meeting us there?"

"Yeah, they'll be there at six. I told Kevin if he got there first to go ahead and get a table for four."

"Did you tell him you were bringing me?" Joni wasn't sure how she would feel if they became a couple in people's eyes. She liked the idea of actually being half of a couple with him, but people assuming they were together when they weren't was something totally different. River's End Ranch was like a small town, and nothing happened without everyone else knowing about it.

"Nope. I like to keep Kevin guessing." He shook his head. "I know it's silly, but he was always the perfect one growing up. If someone else made the honor roll, he made all As. If I made the football team, he was the quarterback. Kevin has always been good at everything he did, and he made me feel lacking."

"Kevin's a good man. I don't know him super well, but I like what I know of him." She looked at him. "This isn't going to be one of those things where you guys try to out-macho each other, is it?"

"Nope. I tried that when we were teenagers, and Kevin would never rise to the bait. He was too good for that, too. That's the thing about Kevin. His goodness is innate. It's not an act at all. It's real."

"I can see where it would be a pain to grow up with someone like that."

"It was! I wasn't exactly known for my good behavior, and Kevin never looked down on those of us who were there for foster care, but he was always the good example. Sometimes I just wanted to mess up his hair so he'd be imperfect."

"So Kevin wasn't one of the foster kids?"

"Yes and no. He was left as a baby on the McClain's doorstep, and he was raised in the house with the brothers." He shook his head. "I think that's why it's so frustrating that he's perfect. He never got into trouble to end up there like the rest of us."

She laughed. "When you meet Bridget, you'll know that he's kept on his toes. She's just a bit too strange to be a pastor's wife. I'm not sure how they fit together, but you know they do. You look at them, and you can see how much they love each other."

"I guess that's good. Of course, it just means Kevin was perfect at finding a wife, like everything else."

"Just wait."

He opened the door to the restaurant, which was in the main building, and she walked inside. It was already noisy, because everyone was gearing up for karaoke. Joni spotted Bridget in a four-top table off to one corner of the room, so she headed that way, taking a seat across from the short woman. "Hey, Bridget." She'd heard that Bridget's sister called her Bridget the midget, and for a second she thought about calling her that, but she didn't know her well enough.

"Hi, Joni. Are you Max's date?" Bridget wasn't one to mince words. If she wanted to know something, she asked it right out.

"Um..." Joni looked over at Max, blushing a bit. She didn't know how to answer that.

"She's here with me." Max wasn't about to say anything else. He was fascinated by the pretty girl beside him, but that didn't mean he was going to announce that they were there together. He knew how small towns worked too well for that.

Kevin looked back and forth between them, nodding a bit. "How's the family? I hate that I missed Adam's wedding."

"Lillian was pretty sad about it, but she understood you were busy."

"I'm glad." Kevin frowned. "She was always so good to me. I wouldn't disappoint her for anything."

"She was good to all of us." He knew Kevin had been special, because he'd been with Lillian since birth, but he also knew she'd never played favorites.

Kevin nodded. "Well, let's eat. I have a feeling there's going to be some serious arguing at this table tonight, and I need to keep my energy up."

Max just grinned. "It's good to see you."

"You too!"

Chapter Three

$\mathbf{T}$he evening proved to be fun—filled with laughter. Max understood now what Joni had meant about Bridget being slightly odd. When she'd demanded to know which Disney princess was his favorite, he'd felt a bit like he'd fallen down a rabbit hole, but he did his best not to let on.

After Max had argued until he was blue in the face trying to get Kevin up on the stage, they walked back toward Max's cabin. "I brought a deck of cards. What do you say we play strip poker, Pastor?"

Joni looked at Max with shock in her eyes, only to find him laughing. "You were joking?" *Please tell me you were joking.* It was hard to believe a man she'd met just hours before thought she'd play strip poker with him.

"I was definitely joking. I like to embarrass the pastor, because...well, probably because I'm evil, but I sure do enjoy it." Max grinned at her, and she shook her head.

"Won't you go to hell for torturing a man of God?" Joni asked, finding it hard to believe that Max would so openly torment a pastor.

"If I will, I was done for a very long time ago!" Max looked over at Kevin, who was shaking his head and laughing.

"Does Lillian know you talk that way?" Kevin asked.

"Are you kidding? I'm twenty-eight years old, and I still think she'd wash my mouth out with soap!"

Kevin frowned at Max. "She never *really* did that!"

"She threatened to once. Told me she was sick of my bad attitude and potty mouth." Max shook his head. He'd had the utmost respect for Lillian, and when he'd realized she had heard him cussing, he'd stopped immediately. "She misses you. She told me to make sure you knew that you're welcome to come home anytime. And you're especially welcome to bring your wife, who she is dying to meet."

Kevin smiled. "I know I am. I don't remember a home before theirs, and it will always be home to me."

Bridget glared. "What am I? Chopped liver? The house we live in together isn't a home? Then what is it? A shack? A dugout?" Max bit back a laugh. Feisty Bridget amused him a great deal.

Kevin just laughed, refusing to rise to the challenge in Bridget's voice. "Have I told you I love you lately, Bridget?"

Bridget sighed heavily. "Not in the last few hours!"

"I'll do better. I promise." He put his arm around his wife and kissed the top of her head.

Max smirked. Bridget was everything Joni had said she'd be and more, but it did seem like Kevin had met his match in her. He couldn't help but be pleased that Kevin seemed so happy.

When they got into his cabin, he found a basket of fruit and assorted chocolates on the counter. "I have snacks!" Max announced, pleased that the ranch had provided something, because he'd had no time to make a run to a grocery store, or any idea where there was one nearby. He could go to the general store, but he had a feeling he'd be happier with the prices at the nearest grocery store.

They didn't end up playing a game, but instead sat around the spacious living room chatting. Joni found herself coupled with Bridget on one end of the room, while Kevin and Max chatted on the other side. Joni couldn't seem to stop looking at Max, watching him helplessly. There was something special about him. Whether he was special enough for the relationship to go anywhere was still unknown.

Bridget started laughing softly. "Max seems like a good guy."

"I don't know about good, but he seems like a fun-loving man, and that's something I think I'm looking for." Joni had always been light-hearted and happy, and she looked for someone who wouldn't bring her down.

"He was one of the foster boys at the ranch, wasn't he? One who moved in when he was a teen?"

"I don't know a lot about it, but he said he moved there as a teen. He never mentioned what he did, and I have a feeling it's none of my business." Joni was curious, but she didn't feel like she had the right to ask.

"Are you going to find out? Do you want me to grill Kevin? I bet I could let you know!"

Joni shook her head, barely resisting rolling her eyes. "If he feels like it's something I should know, then I'm sure he'll tell me. Until then, I need to be satisfied with the knowledge that he's a productive member of society now, and no longer in any kind of trouble."

Bridget wrinkled her nose. "Well, that's no fun at all."

"I don't think looking at the life of a man who was raised in the foster care system should be *enjoyable* for anyone." Joni wasn't sure if she was feeling more upset that Bridget wanted to know about Max in particular, or if she was offended that Bridget was trying to figure out something that was confidential. Either way, she thought Bridget should drop the topic.

"Fine." Bridget leaned against the back of the couch and crossed her arms. "How are Kelsi's babies doing?"

"They're mostly better," Joni said, relieved at the change of subject. "Kelsi thinks she'll be returning to work on Monday, and they'll be going back to the Kids' Korral. I'm sure Debbie is ready to get her hands on them again."

Bridget nodded. "I know when Kelsi brought them to me, they were really sick. I told her to take them to their pediatrician."

"I'm glad you did. They had a mild case of RSV, and I can't imagine how you could have helped them." Bridget was the resident nurse on the ranch, who ran the first aid station, which was hidden inside an apothecary shop in the Old West town. Joni had heard about her doing some good things for injuries on the ranch.

"I couldn't have. My set-up is definitely for adults and the injuries they suffer. I can handle a cold in an adult with no problem, but babies are their own animal."

Joni found herself watching Max again. She just couldn't stop looking at him. "I'm glad one of Kevin's brothers came to visit him."

Bridget grinned. "Yeah, Kevin is really excited. He hasn't seen any of them for several years. The brothers he was actually raised with are busy running the ranch. The others are scattered far and wide, from what I can tell. He was disappointed that he had to do the wedding rehearsal the day Max arrived."

"Max will get over it. We actually went shopping for some winter gear for him while he had the time. He came up here with just a light jacket that was already soaked through." Joni shook her head. "I guess Texan equates to confused about the weather."

"You know I'm a Texan, right?"

Joni nodded emphatically. "And I remember you running around in shorts and a sweatshirt half the winter last year. You finally figured out how to dress for it." The employees of the ranch had enjoyed laughing at Bridget and the way she dressed.

"Did it ever occur to you that I was comfortable in my shorts and a sweatshirt?" Bridget asked, leaning forward.

"No. Were you?"

Bridget sighed. "Not really, but I had a bet going with Kaya..."

"You and your sister are crazy together. You know that, right?" Kaya was the resident romance writer. Her husband had been Wyatt's righthand man until just recently, when he'd opened a therapy ranch for autistic children.

"I do. I'm happy about it, too!" Bridget grinned. "We're super close when we're not trying to kill each other. It's how all true sisters should be."

"I'm glad you think so!" Joni shrugged. "My sisters and I actually get along pretty well."

"I didn't even know you *had* sisters!"

Joni grinned. "They're in the southern part of the state near Pocatello. I usually take a few days off around Thanksgiving and drive down to see them. We do family stuff, and then I come back ready to face another winter on the ranch."

"What kind of family stuff?"

"We do Thanksgiving dinner, and I usually go Black Friday shopping with my sisters. We love to bargain hunt, and we're in line at four in the morning. It's fun!"

"Umm...I think my sister Kaya could do that, because she's still up at four, but I don't think any real person actually gets up that early. It's almost sick!"

Joni laughed. "I'm up that early. Diner opens at six, and I like to run before it opens in the mornings. It makes me feel powerful." She'd always been a morning person, getting up before the sun.

"Powerful? Running?" Bridget shook her head. "Running just makes me feel broken. I don't know why anyone would do it for fun. It's a form of craziness, don't you think?"

"No, I really don't, but thanks for asking."

Pastor Kevin got to his feet. "Come on, Bridget. I have to be up early tomorrow."

Bridget hid a yawn behind her hand. "Me too. I hate mornings."

Joni got to her feet, not sure how anyone would feel about her being there alone with Max. "I should go, too. Four comes awfully early." She hid her grin from Bridget, knowing the other woman would think she was nuts.

She was sure she heard Bridget mumble, "Sick" under her breath on the way out.

Joni grinned at Max. "Bridget hates mornings."

Max looked at the door. "She seems to be rather opinionated about most things, doesn't she? I sure don't see her as a pastor's wife."

"Oh, I don't think she could be under normal circumstances. Can you see Bridget baking cookies and taking them to someone? Or counseling anyone? I think the sky would crash down if she even tried." Joni shook her head. "It only works because we don't have a regular church or congregation here."

"Probably," Max said, shaking his head. "She's something else, that's for sure."

"I warned you!"

"You did. Love really must be blind, because when he writes home about her, we only hear about how beautiful, special, and incredible she is. He never once mentioned her obsession with Disney princesses."

"Bridget has to be experienced to be believed." Joni shrugged. "Thanks for a nice evening. I had fun, though I'm still not sure I believe that Pastor Kevin can sing."

Max raised one eyebrow. "I'll get him to sing before I go, and you'll see."

"Okay. I'm not going to just take your word for it." She pulled her coat on and tugged her gloves over her hands. "I'll see you on Sunday."

"Oh, you'll see me tomorrow. I'm going to come and see what Bob's special is. I know he annoys you, but he's a really good cook!" And he wanted to see her again. She wasn't even gone yet, and he was looking forward to the next day when he'd see her in her ugly uniform, running around like a crazy woman taking orders. What was wrong with him?

"He is. This ranch is lucky to have him, but..."

"Don't tell him you said so! I get it!" He walked out to her car with her, wondering if it was too soon to try to steal a kiss. Back in Texas, he wouldn't have hesitated, but Joni was new to him. She was special, and he didn't want to scare her off. "I'll see you at breakfast time probably. What time does the café open?"

"Six. I'll get there about quarter 'til."

"I'll see you then." He took his hand out of his pocket and rubbed the back of one finger against her cheek. "Your skin is as soft as it looks. I couldn't believe that was even possible, so I had to touch it."

Joni looked up at him, snowflakes on her lashes. The snow wasn't falling hard, but it was steady. "G'night, Max."

"G'night, Joni." He watched as she got into her little beat-up car and drove away. He couldn't help but watch her until her tail lights disappeared. "I think I'm in trouble."

A voice from behind him said, "In trouble? I don't think so. I think you've finally found your way."

Max spun around to see an older woman standing in front of his cabin. That wouldn't have been strange, but she was wearing fairy wings, and she seemed to be walking a rabbit on a leash. "Excuse me?"

The woman began talking again, slowly and exaggerating every syllable. "I. Said. You. Have. Finally. Found. Your. Way."

"Why do you say that?"

"Are you hard of hearing or just a bit dense, boy?"

"Neither, that I know of."

She sighed, shaking her head. "Well, I'm Jaclyn Hardy, and I'm the resident fairy watcher here on the ranch. They help me help others. You, my friend, are here to find your destiny."

"Fairies? My destiny?" Was the woman batty?

She started speaking slowly again. "Yes. Your. Destiny. Do. You. Know. What. Destiny. Means?"

"Of course, I know what destiny means, but I'm not sure why you think I'll find it on a ranch in the middle of nowhere, Idaho."

"Don't dismiss the people you meet here. That's your first mistake, my boy."

Max was getting a little annoyed with how the woman kept referring to him as 'my boy.' It sounded very condescending coming from her lips. "I haven't dismissed anyone."

"Don't. Come see me when you're ready. I live in the house with the gnomes and fairies in the yard." She turned and walked away, trying to keep the rabbit on the leash from hopping off. "Slow down, Mr. Fluffybutt! We're not in a race!"

Max watched her leave, wondering who had just wandered into his life. He'd ask Joni about her the next day. As soon as the thought crossed his mind, he wondered why he thought of her instead of Kevin. *Oh, that's why. Because Kevin doesn't have blond hair and legs that go on forever...*

He turned to go into the cabin and shut the door behind him. As soon as he was inside, he dug through the drawers in the bedroom for the clothes he'd unpacked earlier. Finding his swim trunks, he quickly changed, went into the back of the cabin, and pulled off the cover of the hot tub. He sank into the large tub all the way up to his neck, leaning his head onto the back of the tub.

It took him three minutes to determine that Joni was right. He loved the cool breeze on him and watching the snow fall as he sat outside in a hot tub. This was a good place for him. A good place to think about who he was.

He'd spent the past ten years working for the ranch. He was happy there, no doubt about it. And working there helped him to feel like he was paying the McClains back for all they'd done for him. But was he letting the rest of life pass him by? Was he using the ranch as more of a hiding place? He needed to think on that, because hiding wasn't the answer. He wanted to embrace life...not escape from it.

Of course, the fairy bunny lady didn't seem like she planned to let him avoid anything.

Chapter Four

Max woke early the following morning, as he always did. He changed into shorts and a sweatshirt. He knew Joni would have a fit if she saw him dressed that way, but he needed to run, and he wasn't sure how anyone could run covered in layer upon layer of clothes.

He thought he'd run through the Old West town, along the highway, and then come back in toward the café. He couldn't believe how excited he was to see Joni again, especially since they'd spent most of the day prior together. Never had he been excited to see a woman right after a night out together. He was more of the type who said he'd call after the first date and promptly forgot all about the woman.

He laced up his tennis shoes, absolutely refusing to run in boots. He left his cabin, heading for the route he'd mapped out in his head. As he ran, he inhaled the frigid morning air, thankful that he didn't live in such a cold climate. In Texas, the summers may be as hot as blue blazes, but at least he didn't have to worry about freezing his toes off.

The further he ran, the warmer he became, finally stopping in front of the café just before six. He could see Joni inside setting up her cash register, and he ran in place, doing some light stretches until she came over and unlocked the door. "You could have knocked, and I'd have let you in!" she told him.

Max shrugged. "I needed to cool down anyway. I like running in the cold. Much nicer than running in the summer in Texas."

"Maybe you should try to find a job here on the ranch. I know Glen just left to start a therapy ranch, and he was the right-hand man of our resident horse whisperer."

"I've never worked anywhere but at the ranch. I'm too happy there to even think about living somewhere else."

Joni frowned. She wasn't looking forward to him leaving. Already she felt as if she belonged with this man. "Well, come on in. Do you want me to get you some coffee?"

"Yes, please. Coffee and whatever Bob has for his breakfast special."

"Corned beef hash, two eggs, and three blueberry pancakes," Joni told him. "That good?"

"Sounds great."

"How do you want your eggs?"

"Over-medium is good." He loved to mix the yolks with the corned beef hash.

He watched her as she walked away, enjoying the gentle sway of her hips. After she'd disappeared, he pulled out his phone and checked his email. Nothing. Not surprising. He wasn't the best correspondent, email or written. He didn't enjoy reading and writing letters, so he tended to avoid that sort of thing.

Joni was back a moment later, sliding a cup of coffee in front of him. "Bob's got both of our breakfasts on. You mind if I sit and eat with you?"

"You don't have to wait tables?"

"Nah. No one ever comes this early on Saturday. I really think we should wait to open until seven, but then we'll have someone come in and surprise me."

"I'd love it if you ate with me, then. I had a really good time last night. The ranch is pretty amazing. I ran through the Old West town and along the street this morning. It's so peaceful here that I was simply amazed."

Joni grinned. "I love the ranch. It's the most perfect place in the whole world."

"You should see my ranch in Texas. I love April with the bluebonnets all in bloom. I think it's my favorite time of year."

"But you can't pick huckleberries in Texas. They only grow at high altitudes."

He frowned. "I don't think I've ever even eaten a huckleberry. Are they that good?"

Joni shrugged. "I like them, but I think they're an important part of summer. No idea why. It's just what we do."

"Well, maybe Bob will make me a huckleberry pie."

Joni laughed, shaking her head. "Bob does *not* bake. Instead, he married Miranda. She's the resident baker in the Old West town. You need to go over on kolache day. I swear that woman can make you get down on your knees and beg when she makes them."

"So why doesn't she make them every day? Wouldn't that make sense?" He would think the most popular items would be a daily thing.

"Says they're too time-consuming. Good thing about working with Bob is that she sends some over every kolache day for Bob. He never notices that we each have one before giving him the bag."

Max threw back his head and laughed. "I'm a kolache lover myself. I wonder if she makes them as well as my foster-mom, Lillian. She made them for Sunday morning breakfast when we were growing up, and I would go to sleep every Saturday night drooling." He frowned. "I wonder if she still makes them for the boys, and I just don't get any!"

Joni shook her head at him. "I'd say you were a mess, but I sure do understand being obsessed with kolaches." She looked over her shoulder and saw that Bob had slid the plates through the window. "I'll be right back." She rushed away, grabbing the two plates and the pot of coffee to refill his cup.

She slid his plate in front of him and set hers on the table before refilling his cup. Sitting down across from him, she suddenly felt an overwhelming sense of shyness, which was odd for her. She wasn't used to not feeling confident in every situation. "Did you sleep all right?"

He shrugged. "I never sleep well my first night in a new place. The beds just don't seem to work for me."

"I'm the same way." She took a bit of her eggs. "So what time does your day start in Texas?" She found she wanted to know every single thing about him, and that scared her a little.

He smiled. "I'm always up around four to go for a run before work. It's silly, but I've gotten into that habit over the years. When I first went to the ranch as a teenager, I had way too much energy. Peter, my foster father, made me run in the mornings. It really helped me stay focused in school. I never broke the habit, even though I get more than enough exercise through my work to stay in shape. It just makes it so I can eat two desserts for dinner every night."

She laughed. "I'm a runner, too. I get up at four and run before coming into work, which I love. Doesn't running make you feel powerful?"

He nodded, grinning at her. "Exactly. I feel like I can do anything when I'm running."

"Me too. What time do you start work?"

"I usually have breakfast after my run, and then I start working around six. I could start as late as eight, but I don't want to work as much in the heat. As is, I'm done by about two, and I have the rest of the day in front of me." Max shrugged. "I've found it works better for me than any other schedule, so it's what I do."

"When I was going to school, I had to run early in the morning if I wanted to fit it in. After work was for studying. Now that I'm done, I'm just keeping the schedule." Joni toyed with her fork for a moment. "I'm seriously thinking about applying at your boys' ranch in Texas. I think it would be a good fit for me." That wasn't the whole reason, but she couldn't tell him that she wanted time to get to know him better.

Max felt the excitement rush through him at the idea of her working near him in Texas. They wouldn't see each other at all during the day, but it would be a chance to date and spend time together in the evenings. "I'll talk to Adam and see if he'd be willing to interview you."

"I have a masters in social work. I'd have to get licensed in Texas, but it looks like that would just mean studying Texas laws and taking a test. I've passed the Idaho test, so it shouldn't be a big deal to learn the laws specific to Texas. I can get you a resume to send him if you want."

"Sounds good to me. He'll want you to come for an interview."

Joni frowned. "Kelsi will be back to work Monday. I could probably take a day or two in the next couple of weeks."

"I'll let him know." Max grinned. "Make sure you use Kevin as a character reference. His word will go far in Adam's eyes."

"I'll do that." She finished up her breakfast and leaned back in the booth. "I need to get these dishes to the kitchen and make sure Bob isn't doing something nutty. I'll see you tomorrow after church?"

"What about this afternoon?" His eyes met hers. "I heard there's a movie theater in Riston. There's got to be something out we'd both like to see."

She frowned for a minute, then nodded. "Sure. I usually do my grocery shopping on Saturday afternoons, but I can put that off."

"Are you a creature of habit?"

She nodded. "I'm afraid I am. I don't mind changing things around when it's just my recreation time, but grocery shopping is very specific, and it needs to be done right after work on Saturdays."

"Then I'll go grocery shopping with you. No big deal. Why don't I hit a Red Box, and we'll get a DVD to watch?"

She smiled. "Sounds good. I can fix you dinner at my place."

"Sounds wonderful."

"Any food you don't like?"

"Not really. I'm not a picky eater at all."

"Then I'll make it happen." She stood up and cleared the table. "You want anything else?"

"More coffee? I'm going to sit here for a bit before I walk back to my cabin."

"All right." She whisked the dishes away and took them into the kitchen, leaning against the wall when she got in there. Her heart was beating quickly. "Bob? What should I cook for a man the first time I make dinner for him?"

Bob stared at Joni with a mixture of horror and amusement apparent on his face. "Is take-out an option?"

She glared at him. "Really? That's your answer?"

He sighed. "Is it a guest?"

"Yeah. Pastor Kevin's brother."

"So he's from Texas?"

Joni nodded. "What does that matter?"

"Tells me we want to steer clear of Mexican food and Southern cooking. How about a simple shepherd's pie? I can teach you to make one here so you can just follow my recipe at home."

She sighed. She'd never been known for her cooking prowess, because she had none. "That would work. Should I make a salad to go with it?" Joni had perfected salads, and she could make one in her sleep. She liked to add all sorts of crazy creative things to it, and it always turned out well.

"That would be smart. And for dessert, serve ice cream or something that you don't cook. You don't want to scare him away on the first date." Bob was always blunt to a fault. It didn't make him very lovable, but at least he was able to give good advice.

"Sounds good. Thanks, Bob."

"Pick something up at the bakery for dessert."

She shook her head. "I don't have time to get over there before they close."

Bob pulled his phone from his pocket. "I need an emergency dessert. Fancy as you can make it." There was no greeting, but there was no doubt in Joni's mind he was talking to his wife, Miranda. "Thanks. Delivery?" He ended the call. "Pastor Kevin will bring it over on his way to the wedding he's doing today. He was in line for kolaches."

"Wonderful. Thanks, Bob."

Bob grunted in response. "Come back here at eleven, and I'll show you how to make a shepherd's pie. I'll make a couple of them for a bonus special for the day, and you can make one."

"You're not such an ogre after all."

"Don't believe that for a second. I'm only helping to get you out of my kitchen."

Joni laughed and wandered back to the front of the café. Valerie, one of the other waitresses was in, and she was taking an order from a new table. Lindy and Stephanie would both be in later. Joni went to the other table. "Have you been helped?"

WHEN JONI MET MAX RIGHT after work that afternoon, she had a chocolate cream pie in her hands. "I had Miranda send something over for dessert." Bob's instructions for how to make the shepherd's pie were in her head, and she'd even made one herself under his tutelage.

"Grocery store?" Max asked.

"Why don't you follow me to my place in town? I'll drop off the pie, and then we'll ride together to the grocery store. Does that work for you?"

"Sounds good to me." He didn't like the idea of being in separate cars anyway. "I'll be right behind you."

Joni was a ball of nerves as she drove the twenty minutes to her small home in Riston. She'd shared half of a duplex with her friend Liz, another waitress at the café, until eighteen months before when Liz had married one of the guests and moved to California with him. She missed Liz a lot, but she knew her friend was happy, and that was what really mattered to her.

Pulling into the driveway, she shut the car off and jumped out to put her pie into the fridge. She'd taken a quick peek at it, and it had looked wonderful to her. She hoped it tasted just as good as it looked, because it was awfully pretty.

She hurried back out and met Max at his truck, climbing in beside him. She'd have driven, but she was afraid her car—held together by duct tape and string—might offend him a bit. As a college student, it had been much more important to buy text books than a new car.

She gave him directions to the only grocery store in Riston. When they arrived less than two minutes later, she climbed out of the truck and walked around next to him. "I'm buying all my usual stuff. I like to walk up and down every single aisle. I hope you're all right with that."

He shrugged. "I don't have any kind of preference. I grocery shop when the fridge is empty and there's no longer anything I can cobble together for a meal."

As they wandered through the store, she kept thinking about what Bob had told her to get. It was strange to have Max there with her, but it felt right too.

She ran into Dawna, Glen's younger sister, in the produce aisle. They hugged quickly. "It must be strange for you not working here anymore. How's the ranch coming along?"

Dawna grinned, her eyes excited. "Beautifully. I love working with the kids so much."

"Ranch with kids? Is it a boys' ranch?" Max asked.

Dawna shook her head. "No, it's a therapy ranch for autistic kids. We do equestrian therapy. Glen is amazing!"

"How's Kaya doing now that's it's a working ranch?"

Dawna laughed. "I think she liked it better when it was quiet, but she's doing all right. She keeps odd hours, which makes it a little hard for her, but she says her brain only works to write at night, so she can't do anything about it."

"I remember Liz telling me about Kaya and May and their weird schedules. She could never stay up as late as they did to write with them."

"I still don't understand how they do it! Oh, well. I need to get back. We're baking cookies for the parents of the therapy kids this week. I need to get back before Kaya drifts off into her writer world if I want any help."

"Do you guys do therapy on Saturdays?"

"Yeah, we do. It's a really busy day for us, because school is out."

"Well, have fun, and I'll see you soon, I'm sure."

Dawna nodded with a smile. "In a town the size of Riston, you see everyone you know all the time."

As Dawna hurried off, Joni turned back to Max. "Sorry about that!"

"I know how it is. Our little town is the same way. You can't swing a dead cat without running into someone you know."

Joni wrinkled her nose. "Why would anyone want to swing a dead cat?"

"No idea. Because they're insane, probably." Max grinned at her.

Joni picked up a head of lettuce for her salad, deciding to ignore the "swing a dead cat" statement for now. She wasn't exactly a cat lover, but...it had to be a Texas thing. She'd never heard the expression, and he acted like it was the most normal thing in the world to say. There were lots of cultural differences, even though they'd grown up in the same country.

Chapter Five

Joni and Max got back to her house early enough to start supper. She carefully followed Bob's recipe for the shepherd's pie, adding exactly the spices he'd shown her. Despite what Bob thought, she wasn't a complete imbecile in the kitchen, though she *was* quite inexperienced. She worked at a café and often took dinner home with her rather than messing with cooking. Why would she?

She was stressed out knowing Max was sitting on a stool, watching her cook. Looking up at him, Joni asked, "Do you cook?"

He shook his head emphatically. "I can warm up a pot pie, and my nuking skills are legendary. Actual cooking is completely beyond me."

Immediately she felt better. Maybe she was making dozens of amateur mistakes as she cooked, but he would never know, because he made it sound like he was much worse than she was.

He watched as she cooked, admiring her efficient way in the kitchen. He loved being able to watch her openly. Her long blond hair was pulled into a ponytail, like she'd worn it for work. He'd preferred it when she wore it down the night before, but he couldn't complain too much.

After she'd mashed the potatoes and put them over the meat mixture, she slid the dish into the oven, then started on the salad. Here's where she finally felt comfortable. She efficiently tore the lettuce and added tomatoes, cheese, boiled eggs, and little bits of ham. She loved a salad with everything but the kitchen sink. Before she was done, the salad looked like a work of art.

Max smiled when she added half a box of croutons to the concoction. "You don't make your own croutons? I'm shocked!"

She stuck her tongue out at him as she grated carrots to add to the top. "There." She took out two bowls and put one in front of him. "Salad." She set an array of salad dressings on the counter in front of him.

He stared down at the thing. "You really go all out on your salads, don't you?"

"If there was a way to win the salad Olympics, I would hold several gold medals." Joni stuck her fork into her salad and took a big bite. "No point in doing anything if you're not going to do it right."

He took a bite of the salad and grinned. "I can barely tell there's lettuce in there."

"Is that important to you? To know there's lettuce?"

He shrugged. "Not particularly. Just making a comment." He took another big bite. "Tell me about you. I know you finished school a few months ago, but that's about all I know. How long have you worked at the ranch?"

"I started going to River's End Ranch when I was a girl. My family still comes up every summer. It was our vacation spot. Two weeks every summer, we'd show up with high expectations. When I started my freshman year of college, I did the whole living on campus thing. It took me precisely one week to realize I was not meant for the typical college experience. I didn't want to pledge a sorority. I didn't want to live with strangers and take turns in the shower. I didn't even want to have to share a room." She took a sip of the water in front of her. "So, instead, I decided to see if the ranch was hiring. I finished out my freshman year and applied here for a summer job. I never went back to school and finished through online classes. It worked out so much better for me."

"Why didn't you like living on campus?"

She shrugged. "Snobby roommates top the list. I fit in better here."

Max studied her for a moment before shrugging. "I guess that makes a lot of sense. If you're not of a certain type, I'm sure college can be miserable."

"That first year was for me. After that, I just did my own thing. Most people didn't even realize I was going to school, because I worked a regular shift and just kept going. I'd take finals week off. My school made us be there for finals, but I get two weeks off per year anyway. I used them for finals."

"That's not a week off!"

She shrugged. "It was good enough for me. When was the last time you took a week off?"

"You make a good point. I can't remember my last week off."

The oven buzzer sounded and she went to get the food from the oven. She set it on the stove, eyeing it critically. It wasn't as pretty as Bob's, but it smelled good. She hoped it tasted just as good. "I hope you're hungry!"

"I was until I had that salad!"

She frowned at him, putting her hands on her hips. "Surely you have room for some shepherd's pie!"

"I do!" He watched as she served two big portions and brought him one. "That really does smell good."

"I hope you like it." She sat beside him and crossed her fingers under the counter as he ate his first bite.

"This is really good!"

Joni smiled and took a bite of it herself. It was good. Not quite as good as Bob's, but she would tell the cook it was better, because that's what she did. "Thanks. I made it myself!"

"I watched you, and I have to say I'm impressed. You're better at making this than I am at making microwave burritos, and that's saying something."

"What movie did you pick out for us to watch?" She would be happy with anything if it meant sitting on her couch with him and watching it, but she couldn't tell him that. It might go to his head, and then he'd be like Bob. No one wanted that!

"Have you seen *Wonder Woman* yet?"

"No, and I've been wanting to! Great!"

"What about the new live action *Beauty and the Beast*?"

She shook her head. "I wanted to, but that was right before finals, and there was no way."

"I brought both."

"You're my hero!" She was surprised that she was so excited to see both movies. He'd picked well.

He chuckled, running his hand over the back his neck. "I try hard." He was surprised at how embarrassed he was at her words. He wasn't usually shy around women, but there was something about Joni that was changing him.

She slid off the stool next to the counter and took both of their plates. "I'll shove these in the dishwasher while you get it set up."

He walked to her living room, which was only a few steps from her dining area. The house really was small, and he wasn't sure how she could have lived there with a roommate. "You always seem to be serving me and picking up my dishes after I finish eating."

"It's the sad life of a waitress," she called over the water she had running in the sink. When she finished, she joined him on the couch. "What did you do today other than choose movies?"

He shrugged. "I put on all that cold weather gear you made me wear and walked down to the stables. Did you know they do sleigh rides?"

She laughed, nodding. "Of course. I've lived here for six years."

"Well, I didn't know!" Max shook his head. "I've never been on a sleigh ride, and it's something I've always wanted to do. How 'bout it?"

"How about what?"

"Going on a sleigh ride with me? I hope you'll say yes, because I signed us up for Monday evening."

Joni shook her head at him. "How do you know I won't be sick of you by this time tomorrow?"

He shrugged, starting the movie. "If you are, I'll find some other pretty blonde with legs a mile long to go with me."

"Legs a mile long? That does not sound even a *little bit* attractive."

"Maybe not to you, but to me, it sounds pretty darn wonderful."

She shook her head. "You worry me, Max."

"Why? Because I'm Pastor Kevin's rotten brother? Or because I make you nervous."

Can he tell he makes me nervous? "Because you assume I'm going to spend every spare minute with you. What if I'm on a flight to Texas to interview for a job?"

"I thought I might fly down with you. I have nothing better to do for the next few days." He wasn't sure how she'd react, but he loved the idea of showing her around his home.

"Are you sure that's okay?"

"Oh, yeah. I'll arrange for you to stay a night in the main ranch house, so you don't have to pay for a hotel. It'll be fun."

"Maybe he won't want to interview me anyway."

Max shook his head. "I have influence. I'll get you an interview. It'll be your job to knock it out of the park."

Joni smiled. "That I think I can do." She settled onto the couch with one knee pulled under her and a small lap quilt covering her. The quilt had been a gift from Miranda and her mother when she'd graduated. She wasn't sitting super close to him, but she still felt a smidgeon of awareness. Her heart fluttered. Max was the most handsome man she'd ever been around. There was something about him that made her feel like she was twelve with her first crush all over again.

He used the remote to start the first movie. He'd thought *Wonder Woman* would be a good warm-up movie, and hopefully by the time they got to *Beauty and the Beast*, she'd be feeling all sentimental and maybe she'd relax against him. "Here goes!"

Joni didn't watch a lot of action movies because they made her tense, but she had always been a *Wonder Woman* fan. Her mom had every one of the VCR tapes from the television series, so she'd grown up watching it.

She laughed and cried as she watched, her heart sinking in her chest when she realized who the real villain was.

Max watched her instead of the movie. He found that a great deal more interesting. He'd already seen it anyway.

When it was all over, she slumped in her seat. "I loved it! I feel like they were true to Wonder Woman's story while still telling extra things no one had seen before. It was wonderful!"

He smiled, getting up to take out the first DVD and put in the second. He'd badly wanted to at least hold her hand during the movie, but she'd been sitting so far away. He sat down and rubbed his hands with his arms. "I'm chilly!"

Joni didn't hesitate. She moved closer to him and pushed part of her blanket onto his lap. "I can share."

"Thank you. I like this quilt. Did you make it?"

She shook her head. "No, Bob's wife and her mother made it for me as a graduation gift. It's their thing to make these blankets for everyone."

"Do you know her mother?"

"Oh yeah. She runs the Kids' Korral which is our daycare on the ranch. She recently married Frank, the resident pilot. They're really good together."

"I didn't know the ranch had a pilot! Does he do tours?"

"He does tours, and he flies in people who don't want to make the drive from an airport. He's a good guy." Joni felt his thigh pressed to hers, and she wondered if she should move away a little, but decided against it. The quilt was a lap quilt and not big enough to cover two people unless they were sitting very close.

Max pushed the button to start the second movie, his arm going very naturally around her shoulders. After he'd done it, he was a little surprised with himself. He waited for her to tell him to back off. But she didn't. Instead she snuggled a bit closer to him, her head resting on his shoulder. "I haven't seen this one yet."

"Thanks for being willing to watch *Wonder Woman* with me again."

"Hey, I'm a guy who loved comic books. A superhero movie will never be turned down."

"And I'll never turn down a Disney princess movie, though after talking to Bridget last night, maybe I should."

He laughed. "That girl does like *Cinderella*, doesn't she?"

"No one has ever loved *Cinderella* more, including Prince Charming." Joni tried to keep her face straight as she said it, but she couldn't manage it. "She's just a tad bit daffy."

"A tad bit? In Texas we'd call that girl plumb crazy. One of my brothers would have looked her right in the eye and said, 'Bless your pointy little head.' That always went over well."

Joni laughed hysterically. "Hush, now. I've been waiting months to see this movie."

"Yes, ma'am. Hushing immediately." He wasn't terribly interested in the movie, but he was very happy to sit with her snuggled into his side. He would be content.

Joni loved the movie. She leaned forward to catch little tidbits. When it was over, she sighed. "I loved the new songs. I loved that they gave both Belle and Beast more of a background. It was all wonderful!" She turned to him, tucking one leg under her. "What did you think?"

Like he'd watched any part of the movie when she was so entertaining. "I loved it. It was fun."

"Really?"

He shrugged. "I loved watching you love it. Is that good enough?"

She blushed, looking down. "I didn't realize I was going to be your entertainment for the night."

"Neither did I, but there's no way I'd have enjoyed the movie half as much." He reached out and cupped her cheek in one hand. "I can't remember the last time I had that much fun not watching a movie."

"Is that so?" Joni shook her head. "Why get it if you didn't care to see it?"

"Oh, I wouldn't have minded watching it, but I loved watching you watch it. Was a good night all around."

"Are we still meeting after church tomorrow so I can show you around the ranch?" She had to change the subject before her face burned right off.

"If you're still free." He felt a bit guilty that he'd spent so little time with Kevin, but he knew Kevin would understand. He'd always been the most understanding of guys. Of course, that's how perfect men were.

"I'm still free. Do you want to go out for lunch first?"

She nodded. "That would be fun. I could also pack a picnic, but I think lunch out would be nice too."

"Let me buy you lunch, and then we'll see about the exploration." He ran the pad of his thumb over her lips. "Am I allowed to kiss you goodnight?"

She looked up into his eyes, brown as could be. They made her stomach do flips under her shirt. "What would you do if I said no?"

"I'd respect your wishes, but my lips would go home sad and lonely."

She giggled softly. "Well, we can't let your lips be sad and lonely, now can we?"

He leaned down and gently brushed his lips against hers. He wanted to stay forever, but he sensed she wouldn't like that answer. "G'night, Joni."

"G'night, Max." She followed him toward the door, waiting as he put on his heavy winter coat. "You probably should have warmed up your truck. It's going to be cold!"

He shrugged. "I'm a Texas boy. I can handle a little cold." He leaned down and kissed her once more. "That'll keep me warm through and through." He hurried out into the cold and waved as he hopped up into his truck.

As he drove back to the ranch, his mind was on Joni. He liked her in a way he'd never really cared for a girl. Sure, he'd had a girlfriend in high school that he'd been sure he'd spend the rest of his life with, but what he felt for her paled in comparison. What was it about Joni that drew him? He wasn't sure.

He parked in front of the cabin and jumped down, sticking his hands in his pockets as he hurried to the door. He stopped when he saw the same strange woman, still wearing fairy wings, but the rabbit she was walking this time was gray, and the last one had been black. "Umm...hi."

"Hi. How was your date?"

He frowned. "How did you know I had a date? Were you following me?"

Jaclyn shook her head. "Of course not. I'm not a stalker. The fairies told me you and Joni were going to see each other tonight, and you'd be confused when you got home. Do you want to talk about it?"

Max blinked at her a few times. He was confused, but it had nothing to do with her. Why would she care? "I'm not sure why you're asking me this."

Jaclyn sighed dramatically. "Haven't you been told that I'm the person you go to for matters of the heart on the ranch? The fairies tell me what to tell people, and I tell them. I guess you could say I'm the fairy whisperer, though why they won't just talk to people themselves, I'll never know. I think they like doing things the hard way, but don't you dare tell them I said that!"

"Tell the fairies?"

"I swear you must be hard of hearing or daft, boy! I've never had anyone repeat everything I say the way you do. Have you had your hearing checked lately?"

"My hearing's fine," Max replied, "and I'm not daft. You just say very strange things."

"Of course, I do. I just told you I'm the fairy whisperer, boy! If you can hear, then maybe it's time for you to start listening!"

Max frowned at her. "I've just never heard of a fairy whisperer. A horse whisperer, sure. A dog whisperer, all the time. Even a baby whisperer. But a fairy whisperer? Maybe you should go talk to Bridget. She believes in Cinderella and fairy godmothers."

Jaclyn laughed. "You wait. You'll come crawling to me on your knees, begging me to talk to the fairies about you. Goodnight, Max. I hope your dreams are pleasant." With that she turned and walked away, the bunny hopping along beside her.

Chapter Six

Joni slipped into a pew at the back of the old-timey chapel in the Old West town. She wasn't sure if the church was a new construct or had been around forever, but either way, it was in perfect shape. It felt like the building Laura Ingalls Wilder would have attended services in when she was young.

She could see the back of Max's head as he sat in the front row on one side of Pastor Kevin while Bridget sat on the pastor's other side. He stood and sang hymns as if he went to church every week. Deep down, Joni hoped that was the case. She knew that a Christian man wasn't perfect, but at least most Christian men tried.

After the sermon, she waited for Max to come for her. She'd brought clothes to change into after lunch, but she'd wanted to look her best for him. Her hair was down around her shoulders for a change, and it had finally behaved. It was hard to make her hair look decent on snowy days, but for once, she'd managed.

She watched him and realized the moment he spotted her. He was talking to Shane, Kelsi's husband, who was there alone. She assumed they wanted to keep the babies away from people and out of the cold for one more day. Max's eyes met hers, his lips curved into a little smile, and her heart started beating faster.

She decided not to run for the front of the church where he was standing, but instead she had a discussion with Glen about how the ranch was going. Kaya hadn't been able to tear herself out of bed, because she'd finished a book around six that morning. Her hours constantly confused Joni, but it wasn't her life to live, so she said nothing.

Finally, Max managed to tear himself away from the sheriff and he meandered toward her. Every step he took made her feel a bit giddier. How had he turned her life upside down in less than forty-eight hours acquaintance? She wasn't sure she'd ever understand.

When he reached her, which seemed to take forever, he stopped in front of her and smiled. "Good morning, Joni."

"Morning, Max."

"Bob's here, so who's cooking at the café?" Max looked around, a slight frown on his face.

"We're closed on Sundays. The Weston siblings have a special dinner there every week."

"So we go to Bob's house for lunch today?" He seemed genuinely upset that he wasn't going to get diner food for lunch.

"We can go to the restaurant for lunch, or we can drive into Riston. There's a new Chinese place that's really good. There are lots of places to eat. The café will be open again tomorrow, and you can eat Bob's food."

"I was going to try the Western burger for lunch today. It has onion rings on it!"

"I know it does." Joni patted his arm. "It will be open tomorrow. I promise."

He frowned, but followed her from the church. "Is it closed on Sundays every week? I think someone should have prepared me for this!"

"Yes, it's closed every Sunday." She patted his arm. "You do know that when you go back to Texas, Bob will stay here."

"But..." He sighed. "I guess I can live without Bob's burgers, but I might be coming here for vacations as often as I can." He looked down at her for a moment. "Especially if I can't lure you back to Texas with me."

"Speaking of me going to Texas, have you talked to Adam yet?" She automatically started walking toward the restaurant, not sure what else to do. He seemed to still be mourning the fact that he wasn't going to get Bob's cooking that day.

"I talked to him before church this morning. He said that he wants to meet you, especially if Kevin will vouch for you. Wants to know if you can interview Wednesday of this week."

"Wow. That's so soon." She bit her lip, thinking about what it would take to get away before nodding. "I'll call Kelsi right now, if you don't mind. That way I can arrange for her to cover my shifts. I'll fly out Tuesday, meet with him Wednesday, and fly back Wednesday evening. Then I only need to miss two days of work."

"I don't mind." He spotted a bench and brushed off the snow that had fallen overnight so they could sit down.

She sat down in the spot he'd cleared, pulling her phone from her pocket and tapping Kelsi's number. "Kelsi, it's Joni. I need to take Tuesday and Wednesday off. I'm going to Texas for a job interview."

"No! You can't leave me!"

Joni frowned. "I have to. I feel like I've given you lots of time. You can train someone to take my place."

"I'm just kidding. That's my way of telling you that you're very valuable, and I'll miss you terribly. I will arrange for the days off. I guess you're flying?" Kelsi asked. Joni could hear one of the babies babbling in the background.

"Yeah. I'll get a flight out of Lewiston on Tuesday and fly back in on Wednesday afternoon. My interview is Wednesday morning."

"For social work?"

"Yes! I'll be going to the ranch where Pastor Kevin grew up. It's a boys' ranch that does foster care." Joni didn't add that Kevin's foster brother was there, trying to lure her away. She wasn't quite sure what Kelsi would think of that.

"All right. Consider it done, and good luck. I'll send some prayers up for you, and tell Jaclyn to have the fairies sprinkle a little extra dust your way."

"I think Jaclyn's fairies are working overtime." Joni grinned. "I'll see you in the morning, boss-lady. And thanks for making this easy for me." She ended the call and looked at Max. "I guess I'm really going to Texas."

"Have you ever been?"

She shook her head. "Never. Should be interesting."

"You'll want to fly into San Antonio. It's an hour and a half from the ranch, but the flights are cheaper. Want me to make the arrangements?"

She nodded. "Sounds good. Just let me know what I owe you, and I'll pay you for it."

"Sounds good." He got to his feet and offered her his hand.

For a moment, Joni wasn't sure she should accept it, because it was almost like taking out a billboard that they were dating in a place as small as Riston, but would that be so bad? They were obviously spending a lot of time in each other's company. Anyone with eyes could see that. Slipping her hand into his, she said, "I'm walking toward the restaurant because you didn't give me your preference."

"That works. Do you think they could get Bob to come in and cook my meal?"

"You're obsessing over Bob's cooking. This isn't good for you or anyone else!"

"I understand why it's not good for me, but why isn't it good for anyone else?"

Joni frowned. "You have to know Bob to understand. He's the best cook I've ever known. He really is fabulous. But if you pay him any kind of compliment, he just kind of looks at you, and tells you you've stated the obvious. He's so annoying and big-headed. He can't know! But if other people find out, it'll get back to him and he'll be impossible to work with."

Max nodded. "I get it. We can love his cooking, but we can't be vocal about it."

"Exactly." She frowned. "Miranda wasn't at church this morning. That's not normal for her. I wonder where she was."

"No idea. I'm a fan of his cooking, not his wife's keeper."

Joni shook her head at him. "You're a pain sometimes, Max Logan."

"It's one of my more endearing qualities."

They got to the restaurant, and they went to an open table in one corner. "It's busy here on Sundays because the café is closed, but Kelsi is adamant about keeping the hours her grandmother had when she first opened it."

"So Kelsi's grandmother was Kelsey as well?"

"Yes! They spelled it differently, though. Our Kelsi spells it with an I. The grandmother was E-Y at the end."

"Ah. I think that makes sense."

Barbie stopped by their table to get their order. After exchanging pleasantries with Joni for a moment, she took their drink orders and gave them time to go over their menus.

"Do you know everyone on the ranch?" Max asked after Barbie walked away.

"I really do. It's like the ranch itself is a very small town. There are some guests whose names I never learn, but usually I get to know them as well. We're a ranch that people come back to year after year, so I've made a point of learning as many names as I can. It helps with the feel of the ranch."

"It really is an amazing place. I didn't understand why Kevin was always going on about how wonderful it was, but I do get it now." He looked at his menu, chose something, and closed it. "I'll have to get the western burger for lunch tomorrow. I'm so annoyed the café is closed today."

"If it was open, I'd have to be working, because the twins can't go back to the Kids' Korral until Monday. I'm the only manager besides Kelsi, which means I'd have to work. I've been working a lot more shifts than usual since the babies were born."

"You talk about Kelsi as if she's a friend, and not just a manager."

"Oh, everyone feels that way about all the Westons, I think. They own the ranch. The kids were just given the deed to the ranch at the Halloween party. Their parents have been holding it over their heads for a very long time. Kelsi and Shane are building a house on part of the land that was given to them."

"That's cool. Did they all grow up here?"

Joni nodded. "I wasn't around then except as a guest, but the way I understand it, the kids were all expected to work on the ranch from a young age. It was a given that it would be theirs someday, but they had to jump through a whole lot of hoops to get there. They've managed to do it, finally. Some of the cousins have even started to hang around a lot."

"That's great. Sounds like they're a big happy family."

"They fight amongst themselves at times, and there are always practical jokes played, but when it comes down to it, the Westons look out for each other. I've never seen a family that I wanted to be part of so badly."

"Wait until you see the McClains." Max took a sip of the water Barbie had brought him. "They're amazing people. They have this huge ranch, and they spend their time making sure kids in foster care who no one else wants are happy. They have turned around kids I never would have thought could stay out of prison. It's amazing to me."

"You have a lot of respect for them, don't you?"

"Think about the respect you have for the Westons, and then think about how it would be if you had been taken in by them when your mother decided you were too difficult to mess with. They opened their home to you, gave you food and clothes, a sense of purpose, and love like you'd never believed was possible. That's what the McClains did for me. I have a lot of respect for them. I always will."

"That's really cool. I can't wait to meet them."

"Oh, and Adam said you could stay with his parents. They still live on the ranch, but they have little to do with the day-to-day operations. Lillian is the best cook in all of Texas."

"Sounds good." Joni felt a little nervous about the trip. She was going to a place she'd never been, staying with strangers, and interviewing for her dream job. How was she supposed to stay calm?

After lunch, they went to the vehicle barn to rent snowmobiles. As an employee, she got a discount, so they weren't much. After spending a few minutes showing him how to ride, they took off toward the lake. Their lake was small enough that it completely froze over in the winter, but she didn't think it was quite frozen enough for them to ride across yet. That wouldn't happen until January or so.

She led the way until he overtook her, laughing as he did. She shook her head, not at all worried about it. If he had to show her he could drive a snowmobile faster than she could, then so be it. She wasn't about to drive crazily, even on the small vehicle.

When Max spotted a small house with statues surrounding it, he stopped, looking at it curiously. He looked over at Joni, who pulled up beside him. "What is this place?"

"Oh, this is Jaclyn's house. She's the manager of the RV park." She didn't add that Jaclyn was the resident matchmaker and fairy-whisperer, because who would believe such a thing? Besides, she was thinking about stopping to see Jaclyn, and she didn't want him to realize who it was if he spotted her.

"You know who I am, Max. We've talked the last two nights. Why are you pretending not to know me?" Jaclyn stood beside them, fairy wings in place. "Park your snowmobiles and come on inside. I have tea and snickerdoodles ready for you. I tried a new recipe. I put toffee in the cookies, and I need you two to let me know if they're good or a failed experiment." She turned and walked toward her house, and Max looked over at Joni with wide eyes.

Joni shut off her machine and obediently stood up. "We can't deny her. She's pretty much the boss of everyone."

"I thought you said she ran the RV park."

"I didn't say she was *really* the boss. She just bosses us all around, and we obey." Joni waited as he got off his snowmobile. "Rumor has it she was the best friend of the first Kelsey, the grandmother of the kids who run this place now. She demands everyone's respect, and we give it."

"She's come to my cabin the past two nights. She's always wearing her fairy wings, and she is walking a rabbit on a leash. Are you supposed to walk rabbits on leashes?" Max shook his head, not wanting to follow, but very curious about the strange woman. He'd been half-afraid he'd made her up.

"What does she say when she comes to see you?"

"She—"

"Will you two quit dawdling? An old woman shouldn't be able to walk that much faster than young people. Do you think I have all day to stand around here and gab with you? Well, I don't. The fairies are ready for me to give you their message, and I'm as obedient to the fairies as always." Jaclyn stood with her hands on her hips, waiting for them, her front door open. Max could see at least a dozen bunnies hopping around her living room.

"I'm sorry, ma'am," he said quietly. No matter how crazy she seemed, he knew enough to respect his elders. Southern manners had been drilled into him from the time he moved to the McClain Ranch.

He walked over and stood next to the couch, looking over at Joni. Where were they supposed to sit? There were at least four bunnies on the couch.

"Just push them off or hold them. Your choice. But if you push them, be gentle. Mrs. Dopeyface just got fixed a couple of days ago, and she's not feeling very well."

Max blinked a couple of times, carefully moving two bunnies to the floor and putting one on his lap. "I didn't know bunnies got fixed, ma'am."

"If I don't want them breeding like bunnies, then I have to get them fixed, don't I?" Jaclyn shook her head, addressing her next comment to Joni. "I'm not sure what you see in this one. He's a bit dense, if you ask me. The fairies do seem to approve, though."

Joni choked on a laugh. "I think he seems fairly intelligent. You just fluster him with your bunnies and fairy wings. I do like how they look, though. Have you decided to always wear them now?"

"Well, I don't wear them to bed or in the bathtub, but I think they're fitting the rest of the time. The fairies told me to be one of them for Halloween, because I'd earned my wings. If I've earned them, well, I'm darn sure going to wear them! Wouldn't you?"

Joni nodded. "Oh, yes, ma'am. If you've earned your wings you should wear them. Fairy or otherwise."

"Well, I brought you two in here to give you a message from the fairies as I said. But first you have to give me your opinion on the snickerdoodles. I've never made them with toffee before, and I'm not sure I like them as much this way. What do you think?"

Joni obediently picked up a cookie and bit into it. "I like it. Maybe not as much as your other cookies, but it's good."

"Max?" Jaclyn asked, obviously wanting his opinion as well.

When Joni looked over at Max, she couldn't hide her laughter. He had four bunnies on his lap, and all of them were vying for his attention. "I don't see how I could possibly get a hand free to try one."

Joni picked up a second cookie and held it out to him. "Here, try it."

Max's eyes were confused as he opened his mouth and accepted a bite of the cookie. "I like it. I haven't tried your other cookies, but these are wonderful."

"Good. Thank you for your opinions. Now are you both ready to hear what the fairies have to say to you?"

Chapter Seven

Joni looked over at Max, wondering how he was taking this whole thing. He looked a bit skeptical, but she really wanted to know what the fairies were saying to them. Maybe it was strange, but she'd heard enough stories about Jaclyn and what the fairies were saying that she *almost* believed the woman really did talk to fairies!

Leaning forward, Joni said, "Yes, please tell us what message they have for us."

Max looked at her as if she'd lost her mind, but he said nothing, instead taking her hand in his and squeezing it. If she believed Jaclyn really did talk to fairies, then he could help her find the right sort of medical help after she got to Texas.

Jaclyn frowned at him for a moment before responding. "The fairies said to embrace new challenges."

Joni frowned. "That's all?" She'd been certain the fairies would have a more interesting message. That was absolutely boring, and not even a bit cryptic. She wanted a cryptic fairy message!

"What were you expecting? Don't travel to anywhere in the South during the full moon?" Jaclyn shook her head. "The fairies tell me what they want to tell me and not a single word more."

"I don't know. I've heard so many people talk about the messages you give them and how much better you make them feel. And then you tell me that I need to embrace new challenges? I kind of feel...well, cheated is the only word I can think of to describe it." Joni didn't want to risk making Jaclyn angry, but she really wanted a better message.

Jaclyn sighed heavily. "Okay, don't use a toaster if there's a blizzard forming in Montana."

"So never, huh?"

Jaclyn laughed. "That's right. Never!"

Joni looked over at Max, who was watching her as one of the bunnies tried to climb up his chest. "I think Max likes your bunnies."

"Oh, I'm sure of it. It's the eccentric old woman wearing fairy wings who talks to fairies he's still trying to figure out." Jaclyn abruptly got to her feet. "Put down the bunnies and go. That's all the fairies had to say to you."

Max carefully set each bunny on the floor, wondering why the creatures seemed to like him so much. "Thank you for the cookies."

Jaclyn nodded. "The fairies told me you needed tea and cookies. I'm glad they weren't wrong, but they never are. Have a good day, you two. Joni, don't get too close to the water. The ice isn't thick enough yet."

Joni wasn't sure why Jaclyn found the warning necessary. She wasn't exactly known for being foolhardy, but she knew she needed to thank her regardless. "Thanks, Jaclyn. I'll be careful."

"Good. I don't know that this guy would be able to handle it if you fell through. I think he might just mourn you for the rest of his life. Sudden deaths do that to a person." Jaclyn looked sad for a moment, as if she was remembering something. "Now go on! I'm done with you."

Joni saw that Max was finally bunny-free, so she stood up. "Thanks for taking the time to give us the fairies' message."

As soon as they were outside, Max looked at Joni. "Please tell me you don't really believe she talks to fairies!"

Joni shrugged. "I don't know what to believe, but I do know that Jaclyn *thinks* she talks to fairies, and that's good enough for me. She doesn't hurt anyone, and she gives good advice if people bother to listen at all." She walked back to her snowmobile and threw one leg over. "I think I want to take you through the Old West town next. I know you've seen some of it, but I want to show you the tree where we all hang ornaments every year. It's beautiful."

Max got onto his machine and fastened his helmet on. "After you."

Joni led him back to where they'd started their day, at the tiny little church where she worshipped most Sundays. She loved being with him, but her mind was on other things today. What Jaclyn said bugged her, as well as thinking about the interview she was about to have...in Texas of all places.

She parked her snowmobile beside the church, and got off to walk through the Old West town. "The whole town is covered with lights every Christmas, and on Christmas Eve, we do a huge tree lighting ceremony. Legend has it that the first Westons to settle on the ranch started the tradition, and now it's shared by Westons, employees, and guests alike. It's my favorite thing."

"Do you stay here for Christmas, then?" Max was surprised by that, because she spoke so highly of her family. He'd have thought she'd want to spend the holidays with them.

"It's strange, because I never thought I'd want to spend the holidays here, but the ranch family becomes your family at Christmas. It doesn't matter if it's your first Christmas here, or your twentieth. We have families of guests that come year after year so they can take part in the ranch festivities, which are pretty amazing."

"And you don't go home to your family?"

She shrugged. "Sometimes they come up for the holidays to see me, but no one really minds if they don't. They know I'm happy here. We usually celebrate Christmas while I'm there for Thanksgiving." She looked over at him. "Who do you celebrate with?"

"I celebrate with the family on our ranch. I can see a lot of similarity between the two places really. I feel like mine is the only family who really cares for me, though. I'm glad you don't feel like that."

"No, I really don't. It's been harder here since my roommate Liz got married and moved away, but I still feel like I'm welcomed by everyone. I love doing the festivities here on the ranch, because even if I am alone for Christmas, it doesn't feel like it."

When they'd finished the tour of the ranch, they returned their snowmobiles. "Are you hungry?" he asked. "I'm not quite ready for this day to end. We could go to the restaurant again, or I'd take you to dinner somewhere in town. Whatever sounds good to you."

She frowned for a moment, thinking about it. "I am hungry. Let's go get some dinner."

He grinned, catching her hand and pulling her toward his truck. "I think I want to get off the ranch. Where's a nice place to go?"

"There are a couple of places in Riston, but there's a good steak place in Post Falls, if that sounds good."

"Sounds wonderful. Can you direct me, or should I set up my GPS?"

Joni climbed into her side of the truck and buckled. "I can direct you." She didn't know about him, but she wanted this night to never end. "It's thirty minutes. Is that too far?"

"Not at all. Just make sure you let me know which way to turn."

"Left out of the ranch, and then left at the first four-way stop." After he'd turned, she said, "Now it's straight for about twenty minutes."

"All right. You want music or talk?"

"Talk. Tell me about your mother."

He frowned. "That's not a topic I really like."

"All right." She was quiet for a moment. What was so bad that he didn't want to talk about them?

He took a deep breath. "All right. My mom was from a rich family, and she got pregnant with me at sixteen. Her parents let her keep living with them, but they weren't super excited about being grandparents."

"I see."

"But by living there, she didn't have to work. She never told anyone who my father was, including me, but she went through lots of boyfriends. When I was five, she moved out with one of them. He wasn't a good man. He drank a lot, and he liked to hit both of us. She stayed with him for five years. And then went on to someone worse.

Each of the men she chose was violent and just plain mean. I never really liked any of them." He glanced at her to see if she was listening and then turned back to the road. "When I was twelve, she hooked up with this guy who was dealing drugs. He started using me to make some of the drops. When I was fourteen, I got caught by the police, and they put me in juvie for a bit. When I got out, my mother was gone from him and had signed over custody to the state. So I ended up on the ranch."

"What about your grandparents? Have you seen them again?" Her heart ached for him. It wasn't that he'd been a delinquent. Well, it didn't sound like it to her. It just sounded like he'd been a victim of circumstance.

He shrugged. "I haven't tried to find them. I figure they're glad to have me out of their lives."

"I doubt it. Maybe you should call them. See if they are interested in seeing who you've become. I can't imagine that after living with you for your first five years they weren't attached."

"I have very few memories of them. I know when we left, they said not to come back, so I never did."

"We live in the age of the internet. Why not find an email address and shoot them a message? Or find them on Facebook. Do you know their names?"

He nodded. "I do. I just don't think they'd want to see me."

She decided to drop it, but she knew she wouldn't drop it forever. She wanted him to have family who loved him, and it sounded like he could have that with the grandparents he'd all but forgotten. "So what's Christmas like on your ranch?"

"It's wonderful. The boys all get new jeans. They usually just get jeans from the church that sponsors them, so new is special. Lillian makes a huge feast and the boys come to the house in shifts to eat it. I really don't know how she does it, even knowing she has three ovens. Then each boy is given a handmade gift by one of the McClain brothers who feels particularly close to him. The boys exchange gifts with each other too. They get paid for the work they do on the ranch, and every dime is saved for them. It's pretty incredible."

"So money was saved for you?"

He nodded. "When I finished school, I found out a trust fund had been set up for me. I don't know how the McClains do it, but they put any money that's extra from their big fundraiser every year into funds for the boys. They must do really well at the fundraiser, because I had a very nice portfolio." He shrugged. "Still do. I've never touched it, and it's continued to grow."

She smiled. "That's really cool. It's hard to believe they do so much for boys they aren't biologically related to."

"That's what's so amazing. You feel as if you *are* biologically related after a little while. It's like you're growing up with thirty other boys, and you think nothing of it. I can't imagine living anywhere else."

"It really does sound wonderful. I think I'd feel right at home on that ranch, just as quickly as I did here. Which of course doesn't mean I won't miss my friends here. It's hard to think of what life would be without the café every day, but I'm not going to waste the degree I spent seven years getting."

By the time they'd finished dinner, she had a plan in her head for finding a way to contact his grandparents. She loved the idea of helping him connect with them. She just had to figure out a way to get their names...maybe she could ask around when she was visiting Texas for her interview. Surely someone at the ranch could help her.

When he dropped her off at her car, he leaned over and brushed his lips against hers, kissing her for the first time all day. "I've been waiting to do that, you know."

She smiled. "You could have done it sooner. I wouldn't have stopped you. I kind of like it when you kiss me."

"Oh, yeah?"

She nodded emphatically. "Yup."

"Well, I'll consider doing it more often, then."

"If you have to consider it, then it must not be as pleasant for you as it is for me." Joni sighed. "Story of my life! Don't worry...you don't have to kiss me anymore."

He laughed, pulling her closer to him. "Try and stop me." His lips caught hers again, toying with them softly. "Okay, get out of my truck. I'll see you for breakfast in the morning. Don't forget you're going on a sleigh ride with me. I need someone to hold my hand and keep me safe."

"And in between, I'll be packing for my trip to Texas. Don't forget you said you'd make the arrangements for me."

"I'll give you the flight information when I get to the café in the morning." Max pulled his phone from his pocket. "Oh, first I need your full name, date of birth, address, phone number, and all that good personal stuff."

She gave him the information, and he typed it into his phone with his thumbs. "Now, can I go? I have to get up really early, you know. Not all of us are on vacation."

"Go! I'll see you in the morning." Just as she reached for her door handle, he caught her arm and pulled her in for another kiss. "Now you can go."

"G'night, Max."

"G'night, Joni." He watched her as she got out of the truck and hurried to her old beat-up car. He hoped she wouldn't ever try to take that car very far. Waiting until she'd started the car and pulled out of the parking lot, he drove back to his solitary cabin. It was much more luxurious than where he was used to staying, but he lived in a cabin at home too. Maybe he was just meant for cabins.

As he got out of the truck, he saw Jaclyn hanging around his bushes again, another bunny on a leash. "I'm starting to feel like you're stalking me," he told her.

"Me stalking you! I was here first. You came to the ranch where I live and work and every single night you show up where I'm walking my bunnies, minding my own business. I think you're the one stalking me!"

He sighed, certain he wasn't going to get anywhere trying to talk to the crazy old woman. "Have a good night, Jaclyn."

"Does that mean you're admitting to stalking me?" she asked, stepping toward him. He opened the door to his cabin and shut it softly, hearing her yell, "Come back here! I'm not done with you yet!"

He shook his head and stripped down, putting on his swim trunks. There was something about sitting in his hot tub there on the ranch that he found particularly soothing. He could sit and do it all day. His view of the lake and the mountains behind it was spectacular. It was too dark to see them now, but they had left an imprint on his heart. He could close his eyes and see them.

Before bed, he searched online for the best flight rates for the Texas trip, and booked two flights. He was going to be there when Joni saw Texas for the first time.

EARLY MONDAY MORNING, Max got up, dressed, and went for his run. He wasn't sure if Joni was still working as early as she had been, but he certainly hoped so. When he got to the café, out of breath and sweaty, the door was opened by a blonde who looked like she was a year or two younger than Joni.

"Hungry?" she asked, opening the door wide. "I'm Kelsi Clapper."

"Oh, I talked to your husband Shane at church yesterday. How are the twins?"

Kelsi's face lit up. "They're just fine. I dropped them off at the daycare this morning. Pick a seat, and I'll bring you a menu."

Max looked around the café, hoping to see Joni's smiling face, but she didn't appear to be there. How was he supposed to eat breakfast if she wasn't the one bringing it to him? Even if Bob did make it, he needed her there as well.

When Kelsi pushed the menu toward him, he asked, "What's Bob got for a special today?"

"Breakfast special is breakfast burritos with egg, cheese, potato, and bacon."

"I'll have that and a cup of coffee." Max frowned as he looked around. "What time does Joni work today?"

"Joni?" Kelsi looked at him for a moment, and then her eyes widened. "Oh! You must be Max!"

Max frowned. "How did you figure that out so quickly? You've been home with sick babies, from what I understand."

She shrugged. "Sure, I've been home with sick babies, but this ranch is my home and my livelihood. I know what's going on here, and you're the one who's trying to lure Joni to Texas to work there. Probably good for her, but bad for me." She started to walk away. "And she'll be in within the next fifteen minutes. I usually open alone, and she comes in a few minutes later."

He watched her go with a frown. Were people really talking that much about them already?

Chapter Eight

When Joni parked in front of the café, she didn't see Max's truck. She was a bit disappointed until she remembered that he'd run there on Saturday, so perhaps he'd done the same that day. She had a few minutes before her shift started, so she'd have Bob's special before starting her day.

She groaned when she thought of Bob. She was going to have to tell him how amazing their dinner had been Saturday night, because of his help. He wouldn't fit through the kitchen door, his head would swell so big!

She straightened her ugly polyester uniform and hurried into the café, her gaze immediately going to where Max always sat. Her face lit up as soon as she saw him and she hurried to the kitchen. "Bob, I need your breakfast special for me. And I have to tell you...dinner was fabulous on Saturday. You're not only a great cook, but you're a good teacher."

Bob raised an eyebrow as he looked at her. "Was that so hard?"

"Yes!" She hurried back out of the kitchen, stopping for a minute to talk to Kelsi. "How're the babies?"

"So much better. They're both breathing normally again." Kelsi grinned at her friend. "Tell me about Max!"

"Not with him sitting right there!" Joni shook her head. "You've lost your mind!"

"I heard that!" Max called from the booth where he waited for her.

"Hush you!" Joni called back. "I'm going to go have breakfast with him. I'm not on for another twenty, so I should have time to finish."

"Sounds good. I can handle any crowd we get. I owe you for covering for me. Again."

Joni grinned at her. "I'm happy to do anything I can for those adorable little rug rats."

"They're awfully cute, aren't they? I think little Tori looks just like her auntie Dani, and little Willow looks just like me. Don't you?"

Joni sighed. "Did you forget that you and Dani are identical twins again?"

Kelsi shrugged. "Maybe to the untaught eye."

"I'm going to go sit down with Max now."

"I will do my best to go about business as usual, and not watch you two make cows eyes at each other."

Joni ignored her friend as she slid in across from Max. "Good morning."

Max smiled. "Morning. Kelsi's something else, isn't she?"

"Yes! I'm not sure what that something is, but she's definitely something else."

"I heard that!" Kelsi yelled out. "I'm bringing your breakfast in a minute. Don't get up, Joni."

Joni shook her head. "Did you get my ticket?"

"I did. You're round trip from Lewiston, with a layover in Salt Lake. You need to be at the Lewiston airport by ten tomorrow morning."

"I can do that." She wasn't sure who she'd have drive her yet, but there were any number of people who would be willing.

"Want me to drop you off? Pick you up?"

"That would be great if you don't mind." She hadn't even considered asking him, but she had no idea why. He was a good guy, and she loved the time they spent together. "Tell me about Adam. How do I impress him?"

He shrugged. "Same way you impressed me. Just be yourself. The ranch needs a social worker, so just talk to him and explain your credentials. And tell him Kevin will vouch for you. It never hurts to have a pastor on your side. Especially one who is known and loved by the family who is hiring you."

"Okay. I'll do my best."

Kelsi interrupted then to slide their plates in front of them. "You're going to love the breakfast burritos. I had Bob put extra jalapeños in mine, so they'd be extra delicious."

Joni shook her head. "Aren't you still nursing? You're going to give those poor babies heartburn."

"Oh, they got my constitution. They love spicy stuff. I give them jalapenos to eat with their cereal every morning." Kelsi walked away with that parting shot.

Joni shook her head. "She doesn't really. Shane would strangle her if she hurt those babies, even if she just burned their mouths."

"I have a hard time picturing the mostly-serious sheriff with Kelsi. She's just a little too wild for him, in my mind."

"Their story is super sweet." She took a sip of the orange juice in front of her. "Kelsi was dating this idiot guy Donn the Dreadful for years. The day she broke up with him, she sheriff came in and asked her out. They were married within two weeks. Turns out he'd been in love with her for years, but he wasn't about to ask another man's girl out."

"I don't know if I could have sat on the sidelines waiting for them to break up if I'd had feelings for her."

Joni shrugged. "The sheriff is a *very* patient man. You should see him with those babies."

Max looked at her for a moment, a thought entering his mind. "Do you want children?"

"I'd like a couple. You?" Had he asked her that because he wanted to get more serious? She wasn't sure, but she really hoped so. There was something special about him.

"I don't know. I'm not sure what kind of parent I would be. I didn't have the best example."

"No, you didn't, but you did have a good example later. Just be the kind of father your foster dad was. You seem to have a lot of love and respect for him, so he must have done something right."

Max nodded. "That's true. I'll think on that." He looked down at the half-eaten burrito he had left. He'd already demolished the first. "These are amazing."

"Bob really can cook. He's as good a cook as he is annoying!"

Bob stuck his head out of the kitchen. "Don't mess with me, Joni, or I won't tell you my secret!"

Joni laughed. "You don't have any secrets, Bob. You're just trying to get me to be quiet."

He smiled, stepping out of the kitchen and behind the counter. "Actually, I do have a secret." He reached into the pocket of his apron and pulled out three bubblegum cigars, one for Kelsi, one for Joni, and one for Max. Kelsi carried the two for Max and Joni over to them. "Miranda's expecting."

Joni grinned at him. "Oh, that's wonderful! Congratulations!"

Bob smiled. "I was starting to think it would never happen. We want a houseful of kids."

"I bet Debbie's walking on air," Kelsi said, referring to Miranda's mother. "This is her first grandchild, right?"

"Oh, yeah. Scott's way too young to be having kids."

"How's Miranda feeling?" Kelsi asked. "I remember my early pregnancy. I couldn't stop throwing up. Or grinning."

Joni laughed. "I remember. You kept stopping random guests you'd never met before to tell them you were pregnant."

"I only did that a couple dozen times." Kelsi laughed. "I think I was the happiest pregnant woman alive."

Bob smiled. "Miranda's pretty happy, but she's also pretty sick. She can't hold anything down at any time of day. Not sure why they call it morning sickness. Seems more like all-day sickness to me." He shrugged. "She'll get through it, and we'll all be happy."

Kelsi nodded. "And you need to have a little girl, so my girls have friends to play with."

Bob shrugged. "Boy or girl. I'll take anything as long as it's not an alien. I'm not really up for parenting an alien."

Joni shook her head. "Imagine the kind of cooking that kid will be able to do. With your cooking genes, and Miranda's baking genes? She's destined for greatness."

Bob grinned, heading back into the kitchen without another word. Kelsi looked at Joni. "I've never seen him so happy. Well, maybe the day he married Miranda, but that was the only time. He's really excited to be a father."

Joni nodded. "He is. I think it's great."

"Me too. I'm so happy he found Miranda."

Max finished his burrito. "I'll be here for lunch, because I need that western burger, and then I'll pick you up at your place around six for dinner and our sleigh ride."

"Sounds good to me." She stood up and cleared their table. "I'll see you soon."

He leaned down and kissed her cheek, the first time he'd been that demonstrative in public, surprising her. After he was gone, she was still standing in the middle of the café with her arms full of dishes, staring after him.

Kelsi laughed. "You've got it bad, girl. Have you talked to Jaclyn yet?"

Joni nodded. "Sure have. I didn't find her particularly helpful, but I talked to her. Max says she's at his house every night with one of her bunnies on a leash."

"Oh, that's awesome." Kelsi walked over to work on filling the ketchup bottles. "Do you need to leave early today to get packed for your trip?"

Joni shook her head. "Nah. I don't have to be at the airport until ten tomorrow morning. I never sleep past four. That gives me plenty of time to get ready."

"Sounds good to me. I hate the idea of losing you, but if you can find something in social work, I think it's great. You've been more patient than I deserve, sticking around to help out here until I was ready to work full-time with the twins. I'm ready. It's time for you to do what you went to school for all those years to do."

"That's what I'm going to miss most about River's End Ranch when I finally leave..."

"What's that?" Kelsi asked.

"The constant support and love I feel from my coworkers and friends. You're an amazing woman, Kelsi. I don't care *what* Bigfoot says about you." Joni winked as she walked off, carrying the dishes into the kitchen.

MAX SPENT MOST OF THE day with Kevin. It was nice to just have some guy time with his friend. They talked baseball, Bridget, football, Disney princesses, and even a little bit of Joni.

"So how serious are you and Joni getting? Your names are linked in all the ranch gossip these days. If you're looking for someone to perform a quick wedding, I'm your man." Kevin grinned at Max.

Max looked at Kevin, completely baffled. "I've had girlfriends before. You know I have, but I've never met anyone quite like Joni. There's something about her that has me wanting to run to the nearest store to buy a ring. I'm doing my best to resist."

Kevin laughed. "Maybe you should stop resisting and get down on one knee. Joni is definitely the kind of girl you want to take home to Lillian. She'll love her."

"I'm not going to marry her to please my foster mother."

"Then marry her to please you. I know it seems really fast, but that's how things are done here. And back home, too, as far as I remember."

Kevin straightened the hymnals in the back of one of the pews. "Tell me about Adam's girl."

"You need to meet her. Tiffani is really great. She's the new fundraising coordinator for the event the ranch does every fall. Super sweet, and Lillian absolutely adores her. All the brothers have accepted her as a new sister. She and Adam are living in one of the cabins built by the first boys on the ranch. They love it there."

"She sounds nice."

"She really is. I don't think Lillian would have been more pleased if she'd handpicked his bride herself. It's cool, because she's working for the ranch too, and she's as devoted to it as Adam is. It makes things easier for everyone involved."

Kevin smiled. "I like that idea. I'm glad he's finally found someone. Now the other brothers need to start finding their brides."

"Once one does something, they all do it." Max shook his head. "I can see why you feel so at home on the ranch here. All the good things about the McClain ranch seem to be replicated right here. It feels a lot like home, if you can ignore the cold, wet, white stuff all over the place."

"I kind of like the snow. I heard you and Joni took snowmobiles out yesterday. Did you have fun?"

"We did. It was great. We ran into Jaclyn. Tell me about her. Does she always wear fairy wings?"

Kevin grinned, shaking his head. "The fairy wings are a new addition. Something about the fairies telling her to dress that way for Halloween, so she knew she'd earned her wings and become one of them, or some such nonsense. Jaclyn is harmless, and she'll help you out if you'll let her."

"You mean she'll help the fairies help me? No, thank you. I don't believe in all that hooey."

"Sure you do. You've seen all kinds of weird stuff happen with the McClains around. I know you didn't live in the big house with them like I did, but let me tell you, there are no people on this planet odder than the McClains. When it comes to hooey, they seem to have written the book."

Max rubbed the back of his neck. He'd seen a lot of unexplainable things around the McClains. He'd even fallen once as a child. Daniel, the fourth brother, had held his hand for a moment. He'd been sure his arm was broken before Daniel had come over, but when Daniel left, there wasn't a mark on him, and the pain was completely gone. It was strange, but the McClains did seem to have strangeness follow them everywhere. "I refuse to even think about it."

Kevin laughed. "Why? It doesn't change anything."

"If I don't know about it, then it didn't happen. Let's change the subject."

"All right. Tell me about some of the boys that are on the ranch these days."

They talked for hours, and Max knew that Kevin, who had seemed perfect as a teenager, had matured to become a good pastor. "Tell me about Bridget. She seems slightly unhinged," Max said.

Kevin laughed. "Oh, she's more than *slightly* unhinged, but I took one look at her and knew she had to be my wife. She resisted for a while, because she couldn't see herself as a pastor's wife."

"I can understand that. Don't ever leave this ranch, because if she tried to be a pastor's wife with a normal congregation, she would crash and burn."

Kevin nodded. "That's very true. Something happened where she wasn't allowed to go back to Sunday School for a while when she was a teenager. I don't quite understand the whole story, and I'm not sure I want to."

"Probably not! She doesn't seem the type to do anything the normal way. She's a twin too right? This place seems to be crawling with twins."

Kevin shrugged. "Just Kelsi and Dani, and now Kelsi's babies. And Kaya and Bridget, but they moved here as adults. They were raised near Fort Worth."

"Texas claims them?"

"They're not that bad. Bridget's a really good nurse, and Kaya's a romance writer. She actually wrote a story about the original Westons who settled this land. I did the research and gave it to her, but she wrote it. Was pretty awesome, really."

"Sounds interesting. I'd like to read it. Well, if it wasn't a romance I would. I'm not reading a romance."

Kevin laughed. "I read it. It wasn't terrible. She named it Mail Order Miracle. I don't know that I'd pick up a romance and just read it for fun, but that one was interesting because it was based on the ranch."

"Someone should write about the history of the McClains. Remember how there was an orphan who married into the family, and her adoptive mother always ran around with peppermint sticks in her cleavage? That was one of my favorite stories." Max had no idea if it had really happened, but if you listened to family lore, the woman had not only existed, she'd driven everyone in the town of Nowhere, Texas absolutely crazy.

"You know, that would be a fun project. If you talk to Kaya about it, she'll offer to go and learn as much as she can. Then Glen would have to kill you, so I would say don't do that."

Max grinned. "Why would Glen have to kill me? Is he the jealous type?"

"Glen? Not at all. He is the type to not like it when his wife leaves for weeks on end, though, and telling those stories would take a while. I don't even know if they're written down anywhere, or if the family just tells the stories from generation to generation."

"Do you think it's a project she'd enjoy, though?"

"Kaya? Oh yeah. She'd sink her teeth into it and not give up until she learned every single detail she could as far back as she could learn."

"She sounds interesting. Are she and Bridget a lot alike?"

Kevin shook his head. "They couldn't be more different. It's hard to believe they're sisters, let alone twins. Kaya is over six feet tall with blond hair."

Max frowned. "Bridget can't be an inch over five feet. And she's dark."

"I know. Their mother swears they were twins, though, and she has no reason to lie to us about it." Kevin got to his feet. "Let's hit the café for lunch. I'm craving a western burger and some fried cheese curds."

"I've been wanting to try a western burger. I was so annoyed when the café was closed yesterday and I couldn't have one. Whose idea was it to close on Sundays?"

"The original Kelsey, from what I understand. She seems like she was quite a woman, too."

Max shook his head. "As long as Joni doesn't think she should start acting crazy to be like them, I'm good."

"You're going to marry her, aren't you?"

Max shrugged. "I don't know. I should probably ask her before I run around announcing that I will."

"Might be a good idea."

When they got to the café, Max went to his regular booth, noticing the place was busier than he'd like. There was a big man at the next table placing his order with Joni. "I want Bob's fried chicken, gravy, mashed potatoes, and biscuits. And don't forget the—"

"Jam?" Joni finished for him with a laugh. "Don't worry Bryan. We all know about your jam habit! I won't forget." She grabbed two menus for Kevin and Max and hurried into the kitchen to communicate the order.

Max smiled as he watched her, pleased that he'd get to spend time with her later. He had to settle for that, because he knew she couldn't sit with him with as busy as the diner was at the moment. Oh, well. At least he'd get his western burger.

Chapter Nine

The following morning, Joni was up at her usual time. She went for her run, then worked on packing. Max had promised to be there by eight to get her to the airport on time.

She was careful about what she packed. It was odd knowing she'd be spending the night with strangers who knew Max so well, but she really didn't want to be out the money for a hotel. From what Max said, there weren't any super close hotels anyway, because the area wasn't exactly metropolitan.

By the time she was packed and had all of her things in order, Max knocked on her door. She hurried over to open it, surprised when he stepped inside, caught her by her waist, and kissed the stuffing out of her. He'd always been careful not to kiss her until the end of the night, but she had no complaints that he'd veered away from his normal course.

After he lifted his head, he winked at her. "Where's your suitcase?"

Mutely, Joni pointed, not sure she was even capable of speech after that kiss. There was just something about Max that kept her stomach in knots and her knees quivering.

Before she knew it, he had her suitcase in his truck and had come back for her. "You coming?"

She nodded, following him out the door. Locking it, she followed him to the truck. She rarely locked her house in Riston, because there was almost no crime to speak of, and she trusted all her neighbors. But she would be away overnight.

Once she was settled into the truck and they were headed toward Lewiston, she finally found her voice. "Thanks for driving me to the airport. Are you going to pick me up as well?"

He glanced over at her as he stopped at a four-way stop on the highway. "Pick you up? I'm going with you! My truck will be at the airport."

"Going with me…but you can't do that!"

"Why not?"

She frowned. "Well, you're on vacation, so you can't go back to where you live and work in the middle of your vacation. It's against all known patterns of the universe! What if the universe implodes because you made one rash decision? Think of the guilt!"

He blinked at her a couple of times before he started driving again, keeping his voice calm. "Universal implosion aside, will you feel better about the whole process if I go with you?"

"Well, yeah, but—"

"Then I'm going, and that's all there is to it. It'll be nice to be out of this snow for a day or two."

She shrugged, not sure how else to handle his comments. "Will you be staying at the big house as well?"

"Nope. I have my cabin there, and I'll stay in it. I love the idea of being able to show you my home—where I live and work. And I can't wait for you to meet the McClains. They're incredible people."

"I love what I've heard about them. Did you ever feel jealous of them? Knowing they had parents who loved them and lived in the big house while you had to live in a cabin?"

He laughed. "The cabins were four-bedroom, four-bathroom homes built in the eighties. The old cabins that the first orphans built still stand, and I live in one today. There was no hardship there. But yeah, I guess I was a little jealous, but more of Kevin than the others. We all knew that Kevin wasn't a biological member of their family, just like we weren't, but Kevin lived with them. He was more a son than the rest of us, and that was hard sometimes."

"I can see that. I'm excited to meet them all."

"You might not get to meet all the brothers. They'll be busy with the boys, but you might meet one or two. Adam just got back from his honeymoon, but I doubt you'll see him and Tiffani at all other than the interview. They're in hiding."

"Well, as many as I can, then. I love the idea of getting to know the people who have been part of your life the longest."

He smiled, reaching over for her hand, which rested on the seat beside them. "You're not going to have a choice."

WHEN THEY LANDED IN San Antonio, Max rented an SUV to take them to the ranch. "I could probably take a car, but I'm used to having four-wheel drive, and I hate going without it," he told Joni as they left the airport.

She was shocked at all the traffic. "This city is way too big for me!"

"Me too," he admitted, merging onto the highway and heading north on I-35. "We'll go through Austin, and then you'll see the countryside. I live thirty minutes or so north of Austin. You'll love it. There are no mountains like in Idaho, but the hill country is still a beautiful place to be."

"I'll reserve judgment until I've seen it with my own eyes." She watched around her as they slowly got out of the bustling city and onto the open road between San Antonio and Austin.

"Do you have any desire to sightsee while you're here? We could do the Alamo, if you want."

"I'd love to see it, but I really don't think we'll have time. If I get the job and move to the ranch, you can take me there. Have you been?"

"Oh yeah." Max shrugged. "Oodles of times. It's a tiny little church, and you wonder how that many people stayed in there for so long. It's very unmemorable, despite the rally cry of the Texas Revolution."

She laughed softly. "I'll definitely need to see it sometime then."

"I'd love to take you. And the Riverwalk is really a nice place to go if you enjoy shopping and history. There's *so much* history in San Antonio."

"Someday, I'll take you up on your offer. I love the idea of seeing all the historical stuff...but for now, I need to keep my brain in the game. I'm pretty nervous about the interview with Adam. This will be my first interview since I started working at the ranch six years ago."

"Well, I'm sure you're going to kill it. Remember you have Kevin and me on your side, and we're a pretty formidable team."

"Just pray for me while I'm in the interview, would you?"

"Sure. But you'll do fine."

When they reached the ranch an hour later, he stopped at the main house. "Come on. Time to meet the people who raised me when no one else wanted me." He got her suitcase from the back and led her to the house, knocking when they reached the door.

It was opened by a woman who looked to be around fifty. She was slender, and her eyes were sparkling and happy. Her blond hair had streaks of white, but she still looked beautiful.

"Max, you're home!" She grabbed Max in a big bear hug. "I hated it when you were driving through those blizzards. I couldn't stop worrying about you."

Max smiled, hugging the small woman back. "I was fine. I pulled over when I needed to, and I made it safely to see Kevin—who sends his love, by the way."

"Did you tell him it's time he brought that wife of his home for me to meet? I'm sure she's sweet as can be, if she caught a man like Kevin."

Max choked on a laugh. "I wouldn't call Bridget sweet, but I will say he loves her, and she seems to love him just as much."

"Good. That's what really matters to me. Are you coming back for supper tonight?"

He nodded. "I'd love to, if you don't mind."

"I never mind. Benjamin and Melissa will be here as well to work on their wedding plans."

"Wait—Ben's already engaged to Melissa? I guess when one of your boys falls in love, the others all have to follow suit?"

Lillian laughed. "I don't think they *have* to, but it wouldn't surprise me if they did."

Max looked baffled for a moment. "Well, I'm going to leave Joni in your capable hands. I'll be back at six for supper." He leaned down and kissed Joni's cheek, and Lillian's eyes widened in understanding. "See you soon."

Joni watched him go, feeling nervous about being alone with this woman who was so important to Max. "Thanks for letting me stay here, Mrs. McClain. I really appreciate it."

"It's Lillian. We don't use last names around here, because there are just too many McClains." She studied Joni for a moment, then turned toward the stairs. "Follow me, and I'll show you the room that will be yours for the night. I'm giving you Adam's old room, because it's the only one with a private bath. I think you'll feel more comfortable there."

"Thank you." Joni followed along behind the older woman, fighting an internal battle. "May I ask you a very private question?"

Lillian frowned at her. "I suppose you can. What is it?"

"Do you have any idea about where Max's grandparents are? When he told me his story, it made me wonder if they wouldn't want to see him. I think he feels like he's missing his roots, if that makes any sense."

Lillian nodded. "It does make sense. His grandparents got in touch with us here at the ranch shortly after he was sent here, but at that point, we weren't allowed to let him have contact with them."

"Did you ever tell him that?" Joni wasn't sure what the repercussions would be for something like that, but she felt Max needed to make friends with his past to be able to have a future."

"I haven't. I will, I promise. Thank you for reminding me of it. It hadn't seemed important to me, but I can see that it would be to Max." Lillian turned and showed Joni the room, opening the different doors to show her where everything was. "If you need anything at all, you be sure to let me know."

"I will. And thank you for listening to me. I know I'm just a stranger to you."

"No, you're Max's girl. I don't need to know anything else to welcome you with open arms. Thanks for coming to the ranch, Joni." With that, Lillian was gone, closing the door behind her.

Joni pulled her interview clothes out of her suitcase and hung them in the closet, hoping the wrinkles would come out after a couple of hours. She'd shower with her skirt and blouse in the bathroom if it came to it, but she really didn't want to have to iron. She hated ironing more than she hated wrinkles.

MAX PUTTERED AROUND his house for a few minutes before heading to the stable. His favorite thing about the ranch had always been the horses, and he needed a good long ride to clear his head. He knew he should probably ask Joni to go with him, but when she was with him, his head was anything but clear. No, he needed time alone with just his gelding for company.

As he rode, he looked out over the cabins that the boys lived in. He thought about what his life had been like when he'd lived there. He shook his head. He was no longer the confused teenage boy who had been sent away. He was a man, and he was very quickly falling in love.

WHEN MAX ARRIVED AT the main house for supper that night, he found Joni and Lillian working side-by-side in the kitchen as if they'd known one another forever. Melissa was sitting on the counter talking to them. Her hair was pulled back in the same dark ponytail she always wore.

Benjamin was in the dining room, talking to Peter in low tones. As soon as Max caught the word "wedding," his ears perked up a bit.

"When are you two tying the knot?" he asked.

"Soon. Very soon," Benjamin told him.

Max settled down at the table with the two McClain men. "Kevin says hi."

"What's his wife like?" Benjamin asked.

Max shook his head, chuckling a bit. "You wouldn't believe me if I told you. She's not who any of us thought Kevin would marry, I promise you that."

"Really? Why do you say that?" Peter asked with a frown.

"Well, she's this tiny little thing. Small enough you just kind of want to scoop her up and put her in your back pocket, and then she opens her mouth. She's the most opinionated little thing I've ever met. And she has this thing where she starts fights with everyone she meets, demanding to know who their favorite Disney princess is. Very odd girl, but she loves Kevin, and Kevin loves her."

Benjamin grinned. "Sounds like he definitely met his match with that one. She's going to keep him hopping."

Peter shrugged. "Any woman who's worth having will keep you hopping. If you're willing to overlook their flaws, then you love them. It's that simple."

Joni came into the room then with Lillian and Melissa. Melissa kept grinning at Benjamin, and when she walked behind him, she trailed her fingers along his shoulder as if she couldn't bear not to touch him.

Joni set a huge platter with chicken fried steak on the table, and Max started drooling. As a native Texan, he considered himself a connoisseur of chicken fried steak, and he knew that Lillian made the best, hands down.

"Lillian, you spoil me!"

Lillian laughed. "I know it's your favorite."

"It is, and I'm thrilled you made it. Joni, you're going to love this stuff."

Joni smiled, taking the seat beside him while Melissa sat beside Benjamin. Lillian and Peter were on either end of the table.

"Will you say the prayer, Max?" Peter asked.

Max nodded, bowing his head. He said a short simple prayer before they all started in on the food.

"Lillian makes the best chicken fried steak in all of Texas."

"Texas?" Benjamin asked. "In all the world!"

Joni watched Benjamin with his new fiancé, who hadn't said a great deal while they were in the kitchen. Lillian had talked about how excited she was to finally be getting daughters in her life after so many sons. Melissa seemed to look at him and smile a lot, obviously thrilled to be marrying him.

"So how did you two meet?" Peter asked Joni.

Joni swallowed the bite of food in her mouth. "I work as a waitress at the café on River's End Ranch. Max came in there on Friday, and I served him. We hit it off, and I showed him the ranch. He told me about a job opening here for a social worker, and I just got my masters in social work in May, so I decided to apply for the job."

Lillian smiled, blotting her mouth with her napkin. "Well, I'm glad you're here. You're the first girl Max has ever brought home for us to meet."

Max was a bit flustered by that comment. "I didn't exactly bring her here for you to meet..."

"Yes, you did! You could have easily dumped her at the airport, and you know one of us would have picked her up there. It would have been no problem. The fact that you felt the need to fly with her is telling."

Joni stole a glance at Max, wondering what he was thinking about all this. She was nervous, because she'd never felt for anyone the way she felt for Max. But what if it was a short holiday romance, destined to be over when he returned to Texas?

"She'd never been to Texas before. There's nothing wrong with me flying back to show it to her." Max was definitely on the defensive, which surprised Joni.

"When are you two heading back to Idaho?" Benjamin asked, and Max sent him a grateful look. Being on the spot with Lillian and Peter was never easy.

"Tomorrow evening. Joni is working Thursday morning bright and early." Max reached over and squeezed Joni's hand under the table. "I'm going to take her for a walk after supper. I've seen her ranch. It's time she saw mine."

Lillian frowned. "It's freezing out there. It's in the low fifties!"

Max laughed. "Joni made me get real winter gear. I'm sure I can dress warm enough for a walk around the ranch."

As soon as Joni had helped clear the table, Lillian shooed her out. "Go on your walk with Max."

"Are you sure? I'm happy to help." Joni didn't feel right just running away with all the dishes that would need to be washed.

"Don't worry about that. Go have fun. You only have one night in Texas. Make the most of it."

Joni hugged the older woman impulsively. "Thank you!" She rushed upstairs to get her coat. When she got back down, Max was waiting for her.

"Are you ready?"

She nodded, her eyes bright. "Show me your ranch."

"Well, it's hard to see after dark, but I'll show you what I can." He immediately started walking toward the boys' cabins, pointing out the picnic area where the boys and employees ate with the family every Friday night. "What I really want to show you is the cabin where I lived when I was first brought here. I don't know why, but it feels like the first real home I ever had."

She frowned, again thinking of his grandparents. "I'm glad you've been happy here."

"I have." He pulled something out of his pocket and handed it to her. "I want you to read that for me."

"What do you mean?"

"Lillian said that my grandparents contacted the ranch shortly after I arrived, but she wasn't allowed to let them have any contact with me. She gave me this envelope with a letter they wrote me years ago. I'm not sure if I'm ready to read it, so you have to read it first."

Joni nodded. "I'll read it and let you know if you want to read it. I can't see well enough to read it here, but I'd be happy to let you know tomorrow."

"I'd like that a lot."

Chapter Ten

As soon as Joni got back to her room, she tore open the envelope to read the letter from Max's grandparents. As she'd suspected, they had never blamed him for what had happened. The letter was touching, and she said a quick prayer that his grandparents were both still in good health. The letter had been written in 2003, so she was a bit concerned, but she decided that he should read the letter either way. He needed to know that no matter how much his mother had messed up, his grandparents loved him.

He'd told her he wanted to meet her for her morning run, so she waited in front of the house at half past four, ready to run. It was in the high forties, but that was the summer temperature early in the morning in the part of Idaho she lived in.

He jogged to her, a wary look on his face. "Did you read it?"

She nodded, handing it to him. "They never blamed you, Max. They wanted to see you all those years ago. I'd bet they still want to see you."

His eyes looked haunted, and for a moment, she thought he'd leave right then. Instead he said, "Let's run."

She nodded, sensing that he wanted to run his troubles away, as she'd done more times than she could count over the years. Together, they ran. They ran across fields and around buildings. They ran across the ranchland.

When they finally returned an hour had passed, and she was gasping for air. "I'll see you later?"

He nodded, running back in the direction of his cabin. As she watched him go, she couldn't help but worry. He'd been so distant. Surely he'd be all right.

Shaking her head, she decided to let him deal with it himself. There was nothing she could do to make things easier, so she needed to go about her business. And her business was the job interview she had coming up in a few hours.

IT WAS JUST AFTER TWO that afternoon when Lillian went upstairs to talk to Joni. "Max is in Dallas. He's going to spend some time with his grandparents. He asked that I have someone take you to the airport."

Joni nodded, understanding but wishing things were different. She'd started Max down this road, and if he needed time with his grandparents before he could spend some with her, then it was her fault. "All right. Thank you."

"He said to give you these." Lillian handed Joni his truck keys.

"No, I can't take them. I'll have someone pick me up and take me back to the ranch. It's really not a problem."

"I thought you'd say that, but he said he doesn't want his truck staying at the airport for an indefinite period of time."

"Oh." Joni could understand where he was coming from. "All right."

"Well, let's go. I don't want you to be late for your flight."

"You're driving me to the airport?" Joni asked, surprised.

"Of course, I am. You love one of my boys, and that means you're mine." Lillian headed for the minivan she still insisted on driving, even though her sons were all grown. "He's going to be all right."

"I know. It's just hard that I can't be with him."

"I'm just thrilled you want to be."

MAX STOOD IN FRONT of the huge house where he'd spent the first five years of his life. He raised his hand to knock, thought better of it, and turned to walk away. He was halfway back to his rental when he realized that he'd been waiting for this day for a long time. He couldn't back out now.

Raising his hand, he knocked on the door, holding his breath as he waited for someone to come. The woman who opened the door wasn't familiar to him, but she was about the right age to be his grandmother. Taking a deep breath, he said, "I'm Max Logan."

The woman stared at him for a moment, tears filling her eyes. "We never thought we'd get to see you again."

Max wanted to run. "I didn't know you wanted to see me until this morning."

She shook her head. "What am I doing keeping you outside on a cold day like this? Come in!" She opened the door wide, and Max walked in, half afraid he'd break something. "To your left is the living room. Have a seat while I call your grandfather. He's at work."

"Oh, don't bother him at work!" Max realized he had no idea what his grandfather even did for a living, but he was sure he was too busy to come home in the middle of the day.

His grandmother stared at him for a moment. "Of course, I'll call him at work. We've prayed every day that you would find your way home to us." She left the room, and he could hear her moving around in another.

He looked around him, surprised at the opulence that surrounded him. He couldn't imagine why his mother had not left him here when she'd left, but he knew if she had, his life would have been much different. Would he have gone to college and worked in the family business? Would he have gone to football camp instead of juvie? There was no way of knowing. All he could do now was keep following the path he was plummeting down and get to know these people.

His grandmother came back into the room. "He'll be here in fifteen minutes. Are you hungry? I could have Annie whip up some lunch?"

He shook his head, certain that if he tried to eat, he'd vomit. "I don't think I can eat at the moment. What should I call you?"

She blinked a couple of times before walking over to sit down beside him. "When you were little you called me Grandma."

He nodded. "Is that what you want me to call you now?"

"I would like nothing more. I'm so glad you're here! I know you were sent to a boys' ranch years ago. How were you treated there?" Her eyes were still moist as she asked. "I hope they weren't cruel."

He shook his head. "That boys' ranch is the best thing that ever happened to me. They treated me with love and respect from the first day onward. I've thought of Lillian and Peter McClain as my parents for more than half my life."

She reached out and grasped his hand, and it felt odd to Max. She didn't seem like someone who had a connection with him. "I'm so glad to hear that. Do you know about your mother?"

"Know what?"

"She died a year ago. Overdose."

Max found he had no emotions over her pronouncement. He was sure that made him a terrible person, but he couldn't feel grief for the woman who had made his life miserable for many years. "I'm sorry for your loss." The words were automatic.

"Yours, too. She was your mother."

He shrugged. "She wrote me off many years ago. I have a mother who loves me very much." Abruptly he got to his feet. "This was a mistake."

"Please don't go, Max. At least let my husband come home and meet you. Then you can go if you want to."

Max frowned, but he sat back down. "I can wait a few more minutes."

"Tell me about you, Max. What do you do for a living? Where do you live? Are you married?"

"I work as a cowboy at the boys' ranch where I went after my mother disowned me. I've found my place in the world there, and I'm happy. I'm not married, but there's a girl...I'm not sure how she feels about me at the moment, but I do know I want to pursue a relationship with her. I took her to meet Peter and Lillian."

"And did they like her?"

He nodded. "Lillian said she felt like she was already her daughter. She lives in Idaho, but I think she's going to move to Texas to work on the ranch."

"How'd you meet a girl in Idaho? It's not one of those online relationships, is it?"

"No. I had some time off, so I drove up there to spend some time with one of my foster brothers. She was the first person I met on the ranch. We haven't known one another very long, but my feelings are strong."

"Let me tell you a little secret about your grandfather and me. We met, and got married less than a week later. We've been married for almost fifty years."

He wasn't sure what to say to that. She seemed to be encouraging him to pursue his relationship with Joni, which pleased him. "That's great." He frowned. "Was my mother an only child?"

"Yes, she was. And we spoiled her beyond belief. It's our fault that she turned out as she did. We should have been stricter." He heard the door open behind him. "Oh, that must be Stanley!"

Max turned to see the man who walked into the room where they were sitting. He was a tall man, with gray hair and blue eyes. "It's nice to meet you, sir."

The man walked around to the front of the couch where Max was sitting with his grandmother. "You look just like her, you know."

Max shook his head. "Do I? It's been over half my lifetime since I last laid eyes on her. I'm afraid I don't remember much." He remembered her yelling, but it was her voice, not her face he remembered.

His grandmother hurried away, while his grandfather simply said, "We'd like you to stay with us for a while."

"I have a job that I don't want to lose." And a girl that I might have already lost by running off this way. "I'm afraid I can't stay."

"If you'll stay with us a week, we'll make sure you're written into our will. You'll be our sole beneficiary."

Max tilted his head to one side. "What do you do, sir?"

"I'm a lawyer. And, please, call me Grandpa like you used to."

"I'm not interested in money. I just wanted to meet you both."

"You'd walk away from millions?"

He shrugged. "I'm more interested in the relationships I have with people around me than money. I have a good trust fund already that I rarely touch."

His grandmother walked back into the room then, holding a framed photograph. She handed him the picture, letting him look at his mother when she wasn't much older than he was.

As he stared at the picture, he realized his grandparents were talking to one another, but he didn't hear them. He couldn't focus on both things. The woman in the photo looked angry. She definitely hadn't been happy around him.

"Would you agree to that, Max?" his grandfather asked.

Max looked up, surprised. "Agree to what?"

"Will you stay for a week so we have a chance to get to know you? In exchange, we'll leave all of our money to that ranch you love so much." His grandmother had a pleading look in her eyes as she asked.

Max frowned for a moment. The McClains had a fundraiser every year to help with the ranch's expenses. He couldn't be certain, but if his grandparents had the kind of money they seemed to have, the ranch would be set for a long time. "I'll do it."

His grandmother clasped her hands together, smiling happily. "You won't regret it!"

TWO WEEKS LATER, MAX called Kelsi at River's End Ranch to get a ride back from the airport. His truck was already there, which left him without a ride.

"I'll have Shane come and get you."

"Thanks." After making the arrangements, he sat down and waited for his flight back to Salt Lake City. He had an overnight layover there, and a flight to Lewiston early the next morning. After two weeks with his grandparents—they'd begged for one more week, and he'd acquiesced—he was ready to get back to the real world. A world where people didn't live in a mansion and didn't have servants. He was ready to go back to his ranch, but he had some unfinished business at River's End first.

Soon. Soon he'd talk to Joni and apologize. Soon he'd be able to go home.

MAX FELT HIS HEART start beating faster as soon as the sheriff drove onto the ranch property and he spotted the café. Joni's car was parked in front of it, so he knew she was there. "Just drop me at the café if you would, Sheriff."

"Happy to." Shane parked in front of the small building and Max got out, grabbing his bag from the backseat.

"I appreciate the ride."

"Anything to help the course of true love."

Max wasn't sure about Joni's feelings, but he knew his own. He was worried she was going to be angry with him, but he didn't know what else to do except apologize and explain the deal his grandparents had made with him.

He saw that his usual booth was empty, and he walked over, sliding in. He took his hat off and laid it on the seat beside him.

Joni watched him walk in and took a deep breath. Kelsi had warned her he was on his way, but she'd had no idea what the impact of seeing him would be until he'd walked into the café. She grabbed a cup of coffee and the coffee pot, taking them both to him and filling his cup. "Want Bob's special?"

Max's eyes met hers. "I would like that a great deal. Do you have a break coming up?"

She nodded, walking back toward the kitchen and telling Bob that she needed two specials. Then she told Kelsi she was taking a quick break, and she walked back to Max, sliding in across from him. "How did it go with your grandparents?"

He searched her eyes, and to his surprise, there was no anger there. Simply compassion and understanding. "You're not mad?"

She frowned. "Why would I be mad?"

"I sort of abandoned you and took off for Dallas with no warning. You had to fly back by yourself. I never called you."

She grinned. "Sounds like you're trying to convince me to be angry with you. If you want, I'm sure I can make it happen."

He laughed softly. "I should have called. I just wanted to explain it all in person...and now that I'm here, I can't think of one word of explanation." He reached out and took her hand in his. "Are you taking the job in Texas?"

She nodded. "Adam said I could finish out the year here and start there on January second."

"So you're coming to the ranch? For sure?"

"For sure. I'm staying here through the end of the year, because I can't imagine how hard it would be to replace me at Christmas time." Her eyes met his. "How long are you here for?"

"I have another two weeks. I want to spend as much time with you as possible."

She nodded. "Sounds good. I wish you could be here for Christmas, but I understand. You need to be with your adopted family as much as I need to be with mine." She jumped up to get their plates and brought them back to the table. "Now, how did it go with your grandparents?"

MAX SPENT THANKSGIVING with Joni and her family, but he refused to shop with them on Black Friday. Instead he stayed home with her father and watched football. All day long. By the end of the day, the two men were bosom buddies, and Joni knew her father wouldn't be happy if they split up.

After the holiday, he drove back to Texas, and she stood, crying as she watched him go. She knew she'd see him as soon as she got to the ranch, though, and there was so much to do before then. She was going to live in one of the small cabins on the ranch, and she had to pack up everything she owned—an entire lifetime of possessions—in just a month. It was good he was leaving as much as it hurt that he had to go.

She jumped into packing and the holiday season at the ranch with both feet, refusing to moan around because she was missing Max. The hard part were the holiday festivities. Always before, she'd thought of the people on the ranch as her family, and that had been enough. Somehow, this year it wasn't.

Still, she did every single activity so she wouldn't think about how lonely she was without him. It was strange—she was just as busy as she'd always been, just as involved with everything she'd always done. But without Max there, she felt empty and alone.

The Christmas Eve service was one of her favorite traditions at the ranch, and she was there, sitting beside Bridget. Somehow Bridget had decided they were best friends, and while she didn't dislike the girl, she found her a bit difficult, especially in large quantities.

Part of the ranch's Christmas tradition was that people would make special ornaments for each other, and they were passed out by the Weston siblings after the service. She watched as people all around her got gifts. When one was placed on her lap, she smiled, assuming Kelsi had made her an ornament so she wouldn't feel left out. Kelsi was the one she'd talked to about her loneliness more than anyone.

She opened the package and found a small jewelry box inside. Joni frowned. This tradition was only for handmade things, not store-bought. She opened the box and gasped. There was a beautiful diamond ring inside. Looking around to see who was watching her, she saw Max kneeling beside her. "Will you do me the great honor of being my wife?"

"What are you doing here?" Joni asked, her voice higher pitched than usual.

"I'm here so you won't be alone on Christmas. Marry me?"

Joni felt the tears coursing down her cheeks as she nodded emphatically. "Of course I'll marry you."

He removed the ring from the box and carefully placed it on her finger. "I love you, Joni Kley."

She leaned down and kissed him softly. "I love you too, Max Logan."

"When?" he asked.

"When what?"

"When are you going to marry me, silly?"

She shrugged. "When do you want to get married? I just realized you were even thinking about this. You've had more time to come up with a wedding date than I have."

"How would you feel about getting married on the thirtieth? It's a Saturday, and I already checked to make sure Kevin was free."

She laughed. "All right. The twenty-ninth it is. I'll get my family up here. I'm sure someone has a wedding dress I can wear. And then when we get to Texas, I can just move into your cabin with you."

"Do you have any idea how happy that will make me?"

Joni looked around then, realizing everyone had been watching and listening to their conversation. "Everyone else okay with the twenty-ninth for the wedding?" she asked loudly.

"Works for me!" Kelsi told her. "Just make it an afternoon wedding so I don't have to take off work. I just lost my assistant manager!"

Max saw Jaclyn standing at the back of the church, her fairy wings in place. She smiled and nodded at him. He nodded back, silently thanking her for her help.